Daredevil Doctors

Brothers, best friends...playboys!

After their brother Mick was left heartbroken at the altar and then suffered a life-changing injury in a tragic accident, brothers Eddie and James Grisham made a pact with him. From now on, they would seize life, take opportunities, chase adventure and—most importantly!—remain bachelors forever. Settling down and having their wings clipped is not an option...

Until one by one they meet their match in the most unlikely of places, and their resolve to remain single is tested... With their hearts opened to new possibilities, could an even more exciting future be on the cards for these daredevils?

Can Eddie's guarded colleague be the one to tame his heart in *Forbidden Nights with the Paramedic*?

And when a beautiful stranger arrives with news James is a father, he must face his fears and his future in *Rebel Doctor's Baby Surprise*.

Both available now!

T0014745

Dear Reader,

Have you read one of my recent books called *Fling with the Doc Next Door*? With it being set in Scotland, along with my wonderful heroine Ella and her gruff but adorable Scottish hero, Logan, I think it might be one of my favorite stories so far. It was also where these two books began, because Ella was the big sister of triplets—Eddie, James and Mick.

After Mick was devastated at being jilted at the altar, these three brothers made a vow to be there for each other through thick and thin. They also vowed to avoid anything that could interfere with that bond and their determination to live their lives to the fullest—like a long-term commitment to any particular woman, for example.

It might not be intentional—or even welcome—but some of these vows are finally, dramatically, crumbling.

For all the gorgeous Grisham brothers. And for three amazing women who are about to change their lives forever.

Happy reading,

Alison xxx

Rebel Doctor's Baby Surprise

ALISON ROBERTS

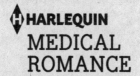

HARLEQUIN
MEDICAL
ROMANCE

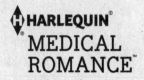

HARLEQUIN®
MEDICAL
ROMANCE™

Recycling programs
for this product may
not exist in your area.

ISBN-13: 978-1-335-59535-5

Rebel Doctor's Baby Surprise

Copyright © 2024 by Alison Roberts

All rights reserved. No part of this book may be used or reproduced in any manner whatsoever without written permission except in the case of brief quotations embodied in critical articles and reviews.

This is a work of fiction. Names, characters, places and incidents are either the product of the author's imagination or are used fictitiously. Any resemblance to actual persons, living or dead, businesses, companies, events or locales is entirely coincidental.

For questions and comments about the quality of this book, please contact us at CustomerService@Harlequin.com.

TM and ® are trademarks of Harlequin Enterprises ULC.

Harlequin Enterprises ULC
22 Adelaide St. West, 41st Floor
Toronto, Ontario M5H 4E3, Canada
www.Harlequin.com

Printed in U.S.A.

Alison Roberts has been lucky enough to live in the South of France for several years recently but is now back in her home country of New Zealand. She is also lucky enough to write for the Harlequin Medical Romance line. A primary school teacher in a former life, she later became a qualified paramedic. She loves to travel and dance, drink champagne, and spend time with her daughter and her friends. Alison Roberts is the author of over one hundred books!

Books by Alison Roberts

Harlequin Medical Romance

Daredevil Doctors

Forbidden Nights with the Paramedic

Morgan Family Medics

Secret Son to Change His Life
How to Rescue the Heart Doctor

Paramedics and Pups

The Italian, His Pup and Me

A Paramedic to Change Her Life
One Weekend in Prague
The Doctor's Christmas Homecoming
Fling with the Doc Next Door
Healed by a Mistletoe Kiss

Visit the Author Profile page
at Harlequin.com for more titles.

CHAPTER ONE

'There's no one home.'

Sarah Harrison climbed back into her car, closing the door very quietly so as not to wake the passenger in the back seat. She also kept her voice low enough to be little more than a whisper.

'I don't know why I'm surprised. He's probably on a full night shift in the emergency department he's working in now.' Sarah made a tiny but disparaging sound with the puff of breath she released. 'And if he's not, he'll be out on a date. He might have only moved here a couple of weeks ago but I'm quite sure he's not spending his nights alone. Leopards never change their spots, do they?'

This was the correct forwarding address, according to the friend who had bent a rule or two to obtain the information for her at a hospital in Edinburgh where he'd been working at, but this ancient, converted barn with stone walls and a slate roof, down a private country lane well outside the city limits of Aberdeen looked like something from the pages of a country house and garden magazine. Sarah had imagined him living in a modern inner-city apartment. A penthouse, perhaps, with a swimming pool or at least a jacuzzi—like any good-looking playboy in a B-grade movie would be housed in?

Sarah leaned her head back and closed her eyes.

She had never been this tired in her entire life and, for a nurse who'd spent over a decade working long shifts in emergency departments that were often stretched to breaking point, that was saying something. Did all new parents feel like this? So exhausted they actually felt unwell?

She caught her bottom lip between her teeth. It didn't matter how hard this was because it was simply what she had to do. What she'd promised to do. And Sarah Harrison had never broken a promise in her life.

But he wasn't home, despite the huge black motorbike parked outside the barn that fitted the image of the man she had come to find far more than the house did. Was he taking a bath, perhaps, and had decided he didn't want to get out to answer the door? No. There weren't enough lights on to make it look like someone was at home. Unless he was in bed? It was a bit early to expect him to be asleep, but maybe he wasn't alone…?

'I'm not sure what to do,' she admitted aloud. 'We've got plenty of time but it'll take us thirty minutes to drive back to the other side of the city and we've got to get home to the B&B before midnight or we'll be locked out.'

It was more than tempting to start the car and drive away. She could come back tomorrow. Or should she go to the Queen Mother's Hospital in Aberdeen instead, and ask for one of their locum consultants to get paged to the reception area? No…she couldn't do that. This had to be kept private because there was the potential for something—or should that be some*one*—to prevent her keeping a promise that was far bigger than the one that had made her drive all the way from Leeds to be parked in front of this seemingly empty house.

If she started the car and drove away she might find an excuse to never come back. She might convince herself that she'd been right all along and this was a very bad idea, despite any perceived rights of another person who didn't realise they were involved. She'd done her best, after all, driving what felt like the length of the whole country to get here. It wasn't her fault he wasn't home.

Starting the car would have another benefit

as well. She could turn the heater on and crank it up. Even though it was warmer than she'd expected driving this far north into Scotland, Sarah felt a chill around her that was cold enough to suggest it was heading straight for her bones. It was also sudden enough to send a shiver down her spine and make her open her eyes and sit up. Sitting here being indecisive wasn't going to help anything, was it?

She reached for her anorak that was neatly folded on the passenger seat and tugged it on. She was about to turn the key in the ignition of her SUV but a sound from the back seat made her freeze.

A small sound. Not much more than a whimper but Sarah felt her heart sink when she twisted her head to see a tiny hand coming over the side of the rear-facing baby capsule. It was a tense hand with spiky fingers, like an angry little starfish.

She checked her watch. 'You're not due for a feed for another forty-three minutes,' she said. 'And I changed your nappy not that long ago…'

But the whimper was turning into a warble. Sarah had to climb out of the car, open the back door and climb in again, because the car seat was anchored in the middle of the back seat.

'Are you cold too, darling? No, you're all

wrapped up like a bug in a rug and your hands are lovely and warm… What's the matter, Button?'

The warble was being punctuated by hiccups and Sarah knew what that meant. Strength was being gathered for some serious screaming to commence.

She undid the safety harness holding the baby in the capsule and scooped her out, picking up the soft, fuzzy blanket to wrap around her. Then Sarah wriggled out of the car carefully. Walking for a few minutes was the best option here, for both of them. That bouncy, rocking walk that could sometimes settle her even when she was really miserable, and a sleeping baby would be preferable to having one that was creating a major distraction in the car when she was driving on unfamiliar rural roads.

A comforting, bouncy walk would help Sarah as well. It had been a lifesaver during the dark days of the last couple of weeks since this baby's mother—and the person Sarah had loved most in the world—had died.

She found herself looking up at the stars as she heard a whisper of Karly's voice.

'I want you to take her, Sass… To look after her…'

'I will... I am already. Ever since you got sick...'

'I know... But I want you to adopt her properly and not just be her appointed guardian Make it legal. Be her real mum...'

'I will...'

'Do you promise...?'

'I promise...'

'Cross your heart and hope to die...?'

Oh, God…the memory of the oath they'd used to cement promises from when they'd sworn eternal friendship on their first day of school together was too poignant now. Sad enough to make the stars overhead nothing more than a blurred streak of light in the inky sky.

Sarah fought back. This so wasn't the time or place to tap back into her grief. She couldn't break down. Not in the middle of nowhere. When she was totally alone.

Except she wasn't totally alone, was she?

They weren't alone.

There were headlights coming towards them down the lane and the shape of the vehicle became very familiar to someone who'd been living in London for so long. Aberdeen clearly had black cabs as well. The driver didn't turn off his lights as he pulled to a stop even though Sarah was standing directly in front of the taxi.

She felt another shiver run down her spine.

She was, quite literally, standing in the spotlight and any second now she would have to explain why she was here. The chance to run away and avoid this confronting situation was rapidly evaporating.

'What the *hell*...?' James Grisham could see the woman with a baby in her arms standing in the glare of the headlights.

The woman sitting beside him in the back of the cab craned her neck so that she could also see what he was staring at. Her suspicious tone was a good match for her scowl. 'Who's that?'

'Never seen her before in my life,' James declared.

'Maybe she's lost,' the cab driver suggested. 'Or having car trouble. Want me to stick around?'

'Aye... Thanks...' James glanced at his companion as he reached for the door. 'You stay here for a minute too, Janine. Just till I see what's going on.'

He got out of the car.

'Are you Dr Grisham?' the stranger asked over the sound of the baby's howling. 'Dr James Grisham?'

'I am.' It was a little disturbing that this woman knew his name. 'And you are...?'

'Sarah Harrison.' She was jiggling the baby

she was holding, turning it away from the glare of the headlights. 'And this is Ivy. Ivy Peters.'

'Ivy doesn't sound very happy.' James was frowning. 'It's rather late to be out and about at this time of night with a wee bairn, isn't it?'

She nodded. 'I've driven up from Leeds to see you. I found a place to stay in the city, but then I thought it might be better to get this over and done with as quickly as possible.'

'I have no idea what you're talking about.'

James narrowed his eyes to take a better look at this woman. Probably in her thirties, he guessed, with a no-fuss hairstyle, parted in the middle and hanging straight down to almost touch her shoulders. Fine features. She looked a bit like a…librarian?

'Do I know you?'

She shook her head this time. 'But you have met a friend of mine. Karly Peters?'

James was echoing her head shake. 'Doesn't ring any bells.'

He heard the taxi door slide open behind him. He caught a whiff of Janine's slightly cloying perfume as she came to stand beside him.

Janine flicked a long tress of blonde hair over her shoulder. 'What's going on?'

'I have no idea,' James said slowly. Whatever it was, however, needed to be over and done with as far as this stranger was concerned and that made it a strong possibility that he wasn't going to like it either.

'It might be better if you take the taxi back into the city, Janine,' he said.

'Oh, Jimmy…' Janine's head tilted as she smiled up at him. 'But you were going to show me your sister's gorgeous house. I adore barn conversions…'

'This is your sister's house?' Sarah was staring at Janine with an expression that was unreadable but definitely not very friendly. Or impressed. 'I was told it was *your* forwarding address.'

'Who told you that?'

'Someone from the general infirmary in Edinburgh. You obviously don't remember meeting Karly, but you did tell her that was where you were working at the time. At that Emergency Medicine and Disaster Management conference in Paris last year?'

Her last words were almost drowned by an increase in the volume of the baby's howls but it didn't stop James from joining the dots with surprising speed. The name Karly was most definitely ringing a bell that was rapidly getting louder. That conference had been about ten months ago. And the baby this woman was holding was an infant that was probably only a few weeks old and had the same surname as Karly. But this had to be a mistake, surely? James couldn't deny he had no complaints about his sex life but he'd always, always been so careful.

No protection was entirely infallible, however. He knew that. Had he really been so confident that he'd never be one of the tiny percentage of failures?

The distraction of the baby crying didn't diminish the triggering of an adrenaline spike that advertised a primitive 'fight or flight' response to the information those dots were hurling in his direction either. If anything, it made it sharper. James could feel his heart skip a beat and speed up. A knot formed in his gut. He could almost feel the prickle of hairs trying to stand up on the back of his neck and down his arms.

Thank goodness his years of working in emergency medicine had taught him how to take control of a potentially catastrophic situation and the first thing to do was to step back from a personal response and look at what needed to happen first.

'Are you sure you've never seen her before?' Janine sounded suspicious now. 'It's more likely you've just forgotten. We all know what you're like…'

'Quite sure,' James said firmly. He put his hands on Janine's shoulders and turned her back to face the taxi. 'But there is obviously something I need to talk to this person about. Thanks for calling me, Janine. I really enjoyed catching up but we'll have to call it a night.'

'But…' Janine was resisting the gentle pressure that was encouraging her towards the open back door of the cab. Her body language was telling James that she was not happy at all. 'I can't believe you're doing this…'

'You did say you'd come up to Aberdeen to visit your grandma,' he reminded her. 'I'm sure she'll be waiting up for you to get home.' He pulled out his wallet and peeled off a bunch of notes to thrust through the front window of the cab.

'I'll get her home safe, don't you worry,' the driver assured him as Janine climbed into the back and slammed the door shut behind her. Then he tapped the side of his nose. 'Never rains but it pours…' He grinned at James. 'Best of luck, mate.'

Good grief… James watched the taillights of the car disappear as it turned into the lane. Had this random taxi driver been joining the same dots?

A shiver got added to the other physical reactions he was collecting.

'You'd better come inside,' he said reluctantly to his surprise visitor. 'It's far too cold out here for a baby. Do you need anything from your car?'

* * *

It wasn't cold inside the barn, despite it being a very large and mostly open-plan space.

A very impressive space with the massive, ancient beams and trusses overhead and the glow of richly polished wooden boards on the floor. The space was broken into distinct areas by the positioning of furniture and what had to be an original interior stone wall that how housed an open fireplace and had a staircase on one side that led to a mezzanine floor. The warm colours in the Persian-style rugs and shelving that was overflowing with books were contributing to the homely feel of this beautiful renovation. So was the heat from the big open fireplace that still had glowing coals in its grate.

It was too warm, actually. Sarah felt a prickle of perspiration on her forehead and realised she needed to get her warm jacket off as soon as possible. She carried Ivy inside and James followed with the baby seat from the car and the big bag of essential baby items that she'd said she might need, even though they wouldn't be staying very long.

'Make yourself comfortable.' James walked past her and put the bag down beside a couch positioned in front of the fire. He shifted the fire screen to put another log onto the coals. 'Can I get you something to drink?'

She *was* thirsty, Sarah realised, but the last thing she wanted was to be sitting here having a cosy cup of tea as if this was a social occasion.

'No, thanks.' She put the still distressed baby on the couch cushions for a moment so that she could peel off her anorak, leaving her with just a light jumper over her shirt. The long boots her jeans were tucked into would have to stay on for now. 'But if you could heat up Ivy's bottle I'd be grateful. It's in the cool pack inside that bag. It's freshly made formula but it'll need heating in a microwave for about thirty seconds. She's not due for a feed for another twenty-five minutes but it's worth a try to see if that's what's bothering her.'

She stared back at the startled glance she got from James. Was he impressed with her well-rehearsed preparations and schedule for Ivy or was he unfamiliar with the best advice on how to care for babies with a predictable routine?

Not that it mattered, but it was probably a good thing that Ivy was making it very obvious that looking after an infant wasn't all cuddles and smiles.

Perhaps the expression on this man's face was more like a shade of shock, in fact. Was it wishful thinking that he was looking rather pale—as if his worst nightmare had just walked up and smacked him in the face?

That might be a good thing too. Sarah had the power to make it go away. To rescue him completely. She only needed his agreement. If Karly hadn't decided to get her solicitor to witness a statement about who Ivy's father was which could be kept with the birth certificate, Sarah wouldn't have needed to be here at all.

'You never know, Sass... Ivy might need a bone marrow transplant one day. Or a kidney. Or she might want to know who her father is when she's old enough to understand.'

'You want her to know that he didn't want anything to do with her? That he offered to help pay to make the whole "problem" go away?'

'You'll think of something nicer to say. You could tell her I didn't know how to find him so he didn't know about her.'

'What happens when she turns up on his doorstep and hears the truth?'

But Karly had been slipping back into a deep, drug-enhanced sleep by then. It wasn't going to be her problem, was it?

Ivy's howling had subsided into a tired sobbing that was heartbreaking. She was also rubbing her nose against Sarah's arm, which meant she was hungry.

'It's coming, darling.' Sarah cuddled her closer and kissed the dark hair that was wispy fine but had been rather distinctively long and lush and inclined to stick up in random spikes from the moment she'd entered the world.

Her father's hair…?

Sarah glanced up as James returned with the bottle of milk. He didn't just hand it her. He sprinkled a few drops of the liquid onto the inside of his wrist, as if he knew about testing it to make sure it wasn't too hot, and he was nodding as he hunkered down in front of the couch so that his head was at the same level as Ivy's and the bottle was within easy reach of Sarah's hand.

She took it but tested the temperature again herself before offering the teat to Ivy. Her little mouth opened instantly and within a few seconds Ivy was making soft grunting sounds with the effort of sucking so hard.

'She sounds like a wee piglet.'

Sarah could hear the smile in James's voice and looked up to find he was looking directly at her. He *was* smiling and there were little crinkles at the corners of his eyes. Dark, dark eyes.

And heaven help her but Sarah could suddenly understand completely why Karly had been mad enough to have a one-night stand with a random stranger when she'd gone to that conference.

James Grisham was undeniably gorgeous-looking.

Fortunately, it wasn't hard to drag her gaze away before she could reveal what she was thinking. Sarah had to adjust her grip on Ivy so she could tuck an annoying strand of her shoulder-length hair behind her ear. Oddly, it felt damp. It wasn't that she was feeling overheated now, though. If anything, she was feeling cold again. Shivery...

'Are you okay?'

'I'm fine.' The response was an automatic reaction to a question like that but the tone of Sarah's voice was much sharper than she'd intended it to be because the concern in James's voice was so unexpected it was shocking. Or maybe it was the feeling that it was so sincere?

Oh, yeah...any woman would fall under this man's spell in record time, wouldn't they?

Sarah could almost feel herself falling, which was ridiculous because men like James Grisham never made it onto her radar of desirable colleagues or potential friends, let alone anything more significant.

Bad boys.

Playboys.

Men who couldn't be trusted with your heart, that was for sure.

Men who couldn't be trusted with caring for a vulnerable infant or raising a precious child either.

'So...' Sarah cleared her throat. 'As you've probably realised, Karly was Ivy's mother.'

'*Was?*' James sounded shocked. 'Past tense?'

'She died last week. Pancreatic cancer. She knew it was a possibility but she put off getting a diagnosis or starting any treatment because she was pregnant and, as I'm sure you know, sometimes it's not even found until it's far too late.'

Sarah was fighting back a wave of grief again. And the 'if only…' accusations.

If only she'd spotted something earlier. If only Karly hadn't been so obsessed with her appearance, which made it normal to notice she was not eating well and/or losing weight again.

James was standing up again. 'That's tragic. I'm so sorry to hear that.' He was rubbing his forehead with his fingers and then Sarah heard him take a deep breath. 'And Karly told you that I'm Ivy's father?'

'She made a formal will after Ivy was born and named me as her testamentary guardian, but she also made a signed and witnessed statement declaring you to be the father. Not that she would tell me anything about you when she discovered she was pregnant.' She could feel frown lines forming on her forehead. 'I could understand why she didn't want you involved.' She scowled at James. 'Did you really think that Karly would go through with a termination just because you offered to pay for it?'

'*Excuse* me…? What on earth makes you think I *knew* that Karly was pregnant?'

Okay…it was very definitely a shocked expression on his face now, but it seemed to be morphing into something far more like anger. Disgust, even…? Sarah hadn't expected this. She'd thought he would simply dismiss the accusation as merely a fact. Nothing to be proud of, perhaps, but also nothing to be particularly ashamed of.

But the expression on James's face was anything but dismissive. 'You think the only involvement I would have wanted was to offer *money*?'

He sounded deeply offended and Sarah's gut instinct was that his reaction was genuine. Come to think of it, if Karly *had* spoken to James or written to him, why hadn't she given Sarah his email address and phone number instead of just telling her where he'd been working? But…this was confusing. She and Karly had never kept secrets from each other.

All her preconceived expectations of what this man would be like were being twisted and turned upside down and that could only make the outcome of this meeting more uncertain. And Sarah didn't like uncertainty in any form.

Anxiety, in addition to the heat in this room, was making Sarah feel slightly dizzy, as if she couldn't catch a coherent thought. To make it even more difficult to think, Ivy jerked her head back from the teat of the bottle, scrunching her face into an outraged glare that suggested Sarah was responsible for whatever had stopped her enjoying her food. Maybe she'd felt the tension escalating in her body?

James was saying something but she couldn't make any sense of his words. Or maybe she wasn't hearing them clearly enough due to Ivy's renewed howling, along with a weird roaring sound in her head.

Oh…*no*…

Sarah knew what was happening now, but it was too late to do anything to prevent it. Her only thought was that she needed to put Ivy somewhere safe, but she couldn't move. She was vaguely aware of James looming over her and taking the baby from her arms.

And then she slipped into the blackness.

The bottle of milk bounced off the couch and onto the floor as James plucked the baby from arms that had gone limp enough for her to be in danger of landing on the floor herself.

He could only watch in dismay as Sarah crumpled and fell back against the cushions, having clearly lost consciousness completely.

Even more disturbingly, James's ability to take

calm control of a potentially catastrophic situation seemed to have suddenly deserted him.

It felt as if someone had just pulled the plug on his life and he was in danger of getting washed down the hole in the dangerous current that had come from nowhere to crash into his life like a tsunami.

He was looking at a complete stranger who could possibly be dying right in front of him.

And he was holding a shrieking baby that was, apparently, his own child.

CHAPTER TWO

IT TOOK A HEARTBEAT.

Maybe two. But then, thank goodness, James rediscovered his ability to deal with this new twist in what already felt like a crisis.

Somehow, he managed to step back from any personal connection. An emotional reaction to the bomb that had just been detonated in his life was inevitable, but it would have to be switched off until further notice. It was Sarah, who was lying there so still and silent, that needed the attention. He tucked the baby into the cushioned interior of her car capsule and covered her with the fuzzy pink blanket that she had been wrapped in.

Within seconds, he'd lifted Sarah's legs up so that she was lying on the couch, removed a cushion and tilted her head back to ensure that her airway was open. He then put the fingers of one hand on her neck to feel for a carotid pulse and the other resting on the bottom of her rib-cage to feel for any movement of her diaphragm that would confirm she was breathing even if it was too shallow to be seen beneath her clothing.

Her heartbeat was rapid but strong and regular enough to be reassuring and she was breathing so at least he knew that she hadn't suffered a sudden cardiac or respiratory arrest that might have been challenging to manage this far away from a clinical facility. Her skin felt damp but hot rather than clammy and it was so pale she looked like a ghost. Not that James knew what was normal for her, of course, having never seen her before in his life. He checked her neck and wrists for a medical alert bracelet or pendant that would warn him of any serious underlying conditions like asthma, epilepsy, heart problems or diabetes but found nothing.

'Sarah? Can you hear me? Open your eyes…' James rubbed his knuckles on her sternum when his voice and shoulder shake failed to get a response, but even a painful stimulus wasn't felt. His mind was automatically flicking through the possible causes for unconsciousness.

She hadn't given any sign of being injured or critically unwell in the few minutes he'd been talking to her so he could rule out a significant head injury or something like blood loss or sepsis for the moment. He would have expected some warning signs, such as a sudden onset severe headache, for an imminent CVA like a ruptured aneurysm as well. He couldn't smell any alcohol fumes and the thought of a drug overdose was just as improbable in someone who took her responsibilities seriously enough to have a baby's routine planned down to the exact minute the next feed was due.

The *baby*...

James turned swiftly as he suddenly realised that the only sounds he could hear were the crackle of the log burning in the fireplace and Sarah's slightly noisy breathing. It was kind of disturbing to find two dark eyes fixed on him. Did the baby somehow realise how serious this situation was and that he was the only person who could do anything to help?

'I'll be right back,' James told Ivy. 'I need to get my first aid kit. Don't move, okay?'

Despite running, leaving the front door open as he went to grab the kit that pretty much filled the boot space of the car in the garage, Ivy was protesting his absence by the time he got back to the couch less than sixty seconds later.

'You're okay,' James told her firmly as he unzipped the pack and opened it on the floor. 'I need to look after your mum.'

Except she wasn't her mum. She was only this baby's mother's friend, who had come to find the man who had been identified as the father and she had something to do that she needed to get over and done with as quickly as possible.

Like leaving the baby with its other biological parent because she'd discovered she didn't really want the responsibility of being this child's guardian for at least the next two decades?

James shook the terrifying thought off, despite the realisation that his protective barriers against having dependents in his life might well have suffered a catastrophic breach. There was something far more urgent he needed to think about. He opened a small case, peeled open the foil covering for a lancet and held Sarah's middle finger to prick it. He fitted a test strip to the blood glucose monitor and then held the other end to the drop of blood that had appeared on her fingertip. It took only seconds for the monitor to beep and confirm his suspicion. The level was too low to record.

Sarah was hypoglycaemic. She was unconscious so he couldn't give her anything oral like food or even a glucose gel. He could give her an injection of glucagon but that was intramuscular and the effects would take too long. Luckily, he carried bags of IV dextrose, so he grabbed everything he needed and arranged it on the floor beside him. If Sarah was diabetic this could be a time-critical situation. If she wasn't, giving her blood sugar a rapid boost wasn't going to do her any harm.

Ivy was still crying but it was a miserable, hiccupping sort of sound that suggested she was too tired to make too much of a fuss.

'I'll be there in a minute,' James told her. 'I have a bit to do here first. See? I'm putting a tourniquet on the arm here and that will make it easy to find a nice big vein. What do you think, Ivy? Shall we go for the antecubital vein in the elbow? Yeah… I agree. And a sixteen-gauge needle? Yes…we want this dextrose to work nice and fast, don't we?'

James swabbed the skin, inserted the cannula and secured it as he was speaking. By the time he was priming the tubing and attaching it to the small bag of solution, he noticed that the baby had fallen silent. Was she listening to him?

No…it seemed that his commentary had been boring enough to send Ivy to sleep. James positioned the IV fluid bag higher on the back of the couch and spent a few minutes taking a full set of vital signs on Sarah. Her blood pressure was higher than he'd expected and her pulse still rapid. She was also running a fever. Had she been feeling so unwell that she hadn't eaten in a long time?

It was more likely that she was a diabetic—possibly a brittle one—and an infection was interfering with her control. If she took insulin or drugs to lower her blood sugar that could well be enough to have tipped her into a dangerously low level. James was debating whether to go out to her vehicle and see if he could find a handbag that might contain clues when Sarah suddenly moved her head from side to side and groaned.

'Oh…no…'

'You're okay.' James put his hand on her arm to stop her bending it and potentially dislodging the cannula, even though the small infusion bag was nearly empty now. 'You've had a hypo. Are you diabetic?'

'Yes…'

Sarah's eyes opened. Quite smartly for someone who was just emerging from a hypoglycaemic episode but everyone was different. Some people would be groggy and confused for up to thirty minutes in a post-ictal phase, but for others it was as if a fully conscious switch had been flicked off and then back on. Sarah Harrison clearly fell into the latter group of patients.

'Where's Ivy?' she demanded.

'Right here beside the couch, in her car seat. Next to your feet. She's safe. And asleep.'

'How long have I been out?' Sarah was trying to sit up.

'Stay still for a minute,' James ordered. 'Your dextrose infusion hasn't quite finished. I'll get you a cushion so you can sit up enough to see Ivy.'

He propped her up with the cushions he'd removed earlier and he could see the wash of relief that went over her face as she spotted the peacefully sleeping infant.

'You've been out for about ten minutes,' he told her. 'I had to get my kit to test your blood glucose level and then get an IV line in. You're going to need something to eat or it could drop again fast, and that's not exactly safe when you're looking after a baby, is it?'

Not *a* baby.

His baby.

'This has never happened before. I use a continuous blood glucose monitor. My phone would have sent an alert if it lost contact with the sensor.' Sarah reached for the pocket of the anorak draped over the arm of the couch but let her breath out in a sound of frustration. 'I must have left my phone in the car.' She pushed up the sleeve of her jumper on her other arm. A small round disc fell onto the couch.

'It's come out.' Sarah sounded shocked. 'Maybe I knocked it when I was putting my jacket on in a hurry in the car.'

'Or maybe your skin has been so damp the cover lost its stickiness.' James picked up the small electronic device with a tiny filament that would have been inserted just under the skin so it could sense and transmit the levels of glucose in the wearer's blood. 'Did you realise you're running a fever? Your temperature's thirty-eight point six.'

Sarah shook her head. 'That might explain why my BGL had gone high enough to need an increase in my insulin dose. I knew I wasn't feeling great today but I thought I was just tired. It was a long drive and I haven't had much sleep and it's been…a pretty rough time…'

Of course it had. She'd lost a friend who was close enough for her to have taken legal responsibility for her baby. James had no right to criticise any of her choices or actions.

'I've had all my vaccinations,' she told him. 'Covid, flu and whooping cough. Even the meningococcal vaccine because diabetes can affect the immune system. I looked up everything and got them all before Ivy was even born because I knew I'd be the one looking after her.'

Already, that level of research, planning and following through on the results wasn't at all surprising about this woman he'd only just met, but James knew the kind of focus needed to keep tight control in type one diabetes. Under normal circumstances, Sarah was probably the perfect patient.

An upward glance showed James that the dextrose infusion was complete. It had done its job well. He disconnected the tubing but didn't want to pull the cannula out until he was sure that the levels were stable.

'I'll do another finger prick,' he said. 'And I'll go and get your phone for you. Have you got another sensor you can put on?'

'Yes. There should be a zip-up cooler pouch on the front passenger seat. That's where I keep my insulin and other supplies.' Sarah held out her hand so that James could extract a drop of blood from her finger.

'You don't use an insulin pump?'

'No. I've tried them on more than one occasion but I prefer the control I get by managing it myself.'

That statement summed up his own impression of this woman so well it almost made him smile. If you wanted something done well, then Sarah Harrison was just the type of person you'd want in charge of it.

'You don't wear a medic alert bracelet either,' he commented. 'I'm sure you know how helpful they can be in an emergency.'

'They can also be very *un*helpful,' Sarah said quietly. 'I don't like people making assumptions that there's something wrong with me or judgements about how I choose to live my life and what I'm capable of achieving. In a medical emergency, checking someone's blood sugar level should be an automatic vital sign to take. It was for you, wasn't it?'

James couldn't argue with that. He could also respect Sarah's right to privacy.

'Back up to four millimoles per litre,' he said as the monitor beeped. 'But I'd be happier if it was higher and we need to make sure it stays there. The dextrose in that infusion will wear off fast. When I've got your phone I'll make you a sandwich so you've got some complex carbohydrates on board. And is there someone I can call for you? A friend or family member that could help?'

'No.' Sarah met his gaze. 'It's just me and Ivy.'

It sounded so final. So…lonely?

'Do you like cheese?'

'Sounds great.' It looked like it was a bit of a struggle to stay awake. 'Thank you.'

It was the first time James had actually noticed her eyes. They were a shade of hazel brown that was the same colour as her hair. They looked darker than they probably were, due to how pale her face still was. And the look in them was… Well, it gave James more than a bit of a squeeze around his heart, to be honest.

Anyone would feel sorry for her. She wasn't remotely hungry, was she? She'd gone through hell in the last goodness knows how long and she was probably feeling ghastly with whatever bug she'd picked up on top of being exhausted, but she was going to do whatever it took to get through this unexpected life obstacle.

Including eating a sandwich that was going to be an ordeal to get through and might not even stay where it was supposed to.

He had to admire that…

There was no point in rousing a soundly sleeping Ivy to give her the rest of her milk and, besides, Sarah was still feeling fragile enough to want to lie back on this comfortable couch and close her eyes for a few minutes while that sandwich was being made. James had given her a good dose of paracetamol to help bring her temperature down so she might start feeling a bit better very soon.

She was horrified that she'd lost consciousness. What would have happened if she hadn't been lucky enough to have been with a doctor who had a well-equipped first aid kit on hand? What if he hadn't come home when he had and she'd gone into a coma parked outside an isolated house miles from anywhere? He hadn't needed to point out how unsafe people might consider her to be as a primary caregiver to a helpless baby. Sarah could feel a growing fear that she might be in trouble here.

That her whole future might be in the hands of this man.

A man who Karly had spent one—apparently spectacular—night with.

A man who, quite possibly, had just saved her life.

With an effort, she managed to swallow a tiny bite of the sandwich she was holding. And then she smiled at James, who was now sitting on the couch on the other side of the fireplace.

'It's a great sandwich,' she said.

There was a gleam in his eyes that told her he knew perfectly well that she was only trying to be polite. 'You're doing well,' he said. 'You'll be halfway through it if you take another bite. Just as well I cut the crusts off, isn't it?'

Sarah could feel her smile widen enough to feel genuine. 'Thank you,' she said quietly. 'And... I'm sorry I ruined date night for you and your girlfriend. I couldn't give you any warning I was coming because I only had an address. I didn't want to find you at work because I thought you'd prefer to keep it private when you found out that...that...'

'That I have a child I knew nothing about?' The tone of James's voice was dry. 'Aye... I should thank *you* for that. Especially when you might have given the hospital grapevine some juicy gossip if someone had overheard you announcing that I'd offered to pay for a termination.'

Sarah ducked her head under the pretext of taking another nibble of her sandwich. It wasn't just a fever that was making her cheeks feel too warm.

'Sorry,' she muttered, giving up on taking that bite of bread that tasted like cardboard and cheese that seemed vaguely soapy. 'But I did believe her at the time, which was why I never tried to persuade Karly to let you know what was going on when she got sick. I was convinced that you were some irresponsible playboy or possibly a sex addict. Either way, it seemed like you were someone who didn't give a damn about any repercussions of failed contraception or brokenhearted women.'

James gave a huff of sound. 'That's a bit harsh,' he murmured. 'And I can assure you that protection was used on my part even after Karly assured me she was on the Pill.'

Oh… Sarah so didn't want to go anywhere near the mental images that were trying to surface here, so she focused on what seemed like another lie Karly had told.

'She wasn't on the Pill,' she said aloud.

'Are you sure about that?'

'We didn't keep secrets from each other.' But Sarah let her breath out in a sigh. 'At least, I didn't think we did. But she did have a thing about avoiding doctors or drugs if she could find an alternative and she'd been adamant that the risk of taking the Pill was too high for her because she had a history of getting migraine headaches.'

'Why would she have said that she was taking it, then?'

'I have no idea. Maybe there's a lot of stuff I didn't know about her.' And she never would now. Sarah had to fight a renewed threat of tears.

James broke the silence that fell. 'How long had you known each other?'

'Since our first day at primary school. We were both five years old. Karly was in a foster home. I was being brought up by my grandmother. Neither of us had any siblings so we decided that day that we would be sisters. For ever.'

James was silent again for a long moment. 'I'm really sorry for your loss,' he said quietly, then. 'I came close to losing one of my brothers not so long ago and that was devastating enough. That's why I've moved up to Aberdeen. Why I'm looking after my sister's house for a while. To be closer to my family—the people that really matter…' He blew out a breath. 'And, just for the record, Janine isn't my girlfriend. She was someone I worked with in Edinburgh and she turned up at work today and wanted to catch up over dinner.'

'She didn't look too happy about being sent home.'

'Possibly. But I can assure you she has absolutely no reason to be broken-hearted.'

The implication was that neither had Karly, and his words felt like a reprimand for the opinion of him that Sarah had unleashed. And fair play. For heaven's sake… She'd had no right to judge him like that. So what if her best friend and some gorgeous guy happened to have been attracted enough to each other to have had a one-night stand when they were a long way away from their normal lives and never likely to see each other again? She would have done the same thing herself, wouldn't she?

Um…no…

But she might have wished she *could* have been more like Karly and made the most of an opportunity like that. She might have discovered that sex didn't have to be so predictable and kind of boring…

Sarah managed another small bite of the sandwich. Maybe the paracetamol was kicking in or her body was happier with its levels of blood sugar because she wasn't feeling quite so awful. Just tired. So tired that all she wanted to do was curl up in front of this fire and sleep for a week.

With Ivy's father watching her and making a judgement call about whether she was competent to be an adoptive parent?

Sarah sat up straighter. 'I should go,' she said. 'I'm feeling much better, thanks to you, and my BGL is high enough for me to be safe to drive. I'm booked in at a B&B in town and I need to be back there before midnight or we'll be locked out.'

James just looked at her. And smiled.

A smile that gave him those crinkles around his eyes again. One that was kind enough to give Sarah such a lump in her throat it felt like a bit of that horrible sandwich. She could feel a tear that had appeared so fast she had no chance to catch it before it rolled down the side of her nose. This wasn't like her at all. How sick and weak was she, to feel this helpless?

Lost, even?

So grateful that some stranger was kind enough to be prepared to look after her?

'The only place you're going, sweetheart,' James said firmly, 'is straight to bed.'

CHAPTER THREE

'HEY, EDDIE…SORRY—did I wake you up?'

'You woke us both up. It's…' The pause suggested that his brother was checking his watch. Or maybe that muffled sound was him apologising to his partner, Jodie, before he rolled out of bed and let her go back to sleep. There might have also been an unmistakable kissing sound. 'It's six-thirty a.m.,' Eddie said clearly, a few seconds later. 'On a day off. What's going on?'

'I just wanted to let you know I'm not going to make that hike we were planning on doing up in the Cairngorms today.'

'Hang on a tick.' James could hear that Eddie was moving. He heard the sound of running water and then a clunk of crockery. 'I need coffee,' Eddie muttered. He'd activated the camera on his phone now but it was propped up on the kitchen bench so all James could see were Eddie's hands spooning coffee into a mug.

James could do with another cup of coffee himself but he couldn't move right now. He was sitting on the couch with a sleeping baby in his arms. An empty milk bottle sat on the arm of the couch and his free hand was now occupied with holding his phone as he spoke to his brother.

'Is the weather forecast bad?' Eddie asked. 'Is that why you're wimping out of the hike? Jodie and I will still go, you know. Even if it's snowing. We like a bit of a challenge.'

'I have no idea what the weather forecast is,' James said. 'I can't go because I've got someone here.'

'Ah…' The sound was drawn out. Amused. 'Overnight visitor, huh? Lucky you. Who is she?'

'Her name's Ivy.'

'And I'm guessing she's still asleep? Worn out?' Eddie face came into view and he was grinning broadly. 'Good to know that you haven't lost your mojo. And that you're settling into your new job so well.'

James felt suddenly weary. He could hear an echo of Janine's accusation last night.

We all know what you're like…

Even a complete stranger who lived in a city he'd never been anywhere near had heard about him.

'It seemed like you were someone who didn't give a damn about any repercussions of failed contraception or broken-hearted women…'

He wasn't that bad, was he? Okay, it might

take a while to do a head count of women whose company he'd enjoyed over the years but he'd only been playing a game that hadn't hurt anyone, as far as he knew. He worked hard. He played hard. He was making the most of his life.

A life that had just had a frighteningly huge bomb hurled into it.

James held the phone further away and tilted it, watching Eddie's face as he saw what he was holding.

'*That's* Ivy…?'

'Aye…'

'Where's Ivy's mother?'

'Not here.'

'Why not?'

'She's dead.'

Eddie nearly choked on the sip of coffee he'd just taken. James listened to his brother swearing, watched the screen image bouncing as a dishcloth was found to wipe the splatters off his phone and then saw the shocked expression as Eddie sank into a chair at his kitchen table.

'Are you telling me you've got a dead person in your house?'

'Good grief, no…it was Ivy's mother's friend who turned up late last night. Her legal guardian, apparently. She'd decided to let me know that I'm Ivy's father, even though Ivy's mum chose not to tell me she was pregnant for some reason.'

Several seconds of shocked silence from Eddie gave James plenty of time for a small voice at the back of his mind to put the knife in.

He knew the reason perfectly well, didn't he? He might have believed that his 'mojo' included being completely honest with women about his status as a committed bachelor but he was more than happy to give them a night they would never forget, Karly—like Janine and God only knew how many others—thought they knew what he was *really* like. She'd convinced her friend that he was an irresponsible playboy and/or a sex addict.

The thought that he might have left women feeling used instead of appreciated was…well, it was shocking, that was what it was.

Almost as shocking as being presented with a small human he might well have contributed to creating.

He'd had a whole night with Ivy now and the shock still hadn't worn off. He wasn't feeling any kind of connection to this baby. It felt like someone else's baby.

Someone else's problem that had just been handed to him.

He'd known for hours that he needed help and he'd waited as long as he could to ring the first available member of his support network, but he couldn't blame his brother Eddie for not being happy about being contacted at this hour of the morning.

He did his best to summon a smile. 'Anyway... I thought I'd share the joy and let you know that you might be an uncle. Not that I've done a DNA test or anything, but I have to admit I had a rather memorable night with Ivy's mother in Paris last year and the timeline fits...'

'Show me again?'

Eddie stared at the sleeping baby for a long, long moment. 'Don't think you need a DNA test,' he said quietly. 'Have you seen that hair?'

'Hard to miss,' James agreed.

'Don't you recognise it?'

'What do you mean?'

'You know that bookshelf under the picture of zebras that Ella's got on the wall? The one that's got photos in gaps between the books?'

'I'm looking at it right now.'

'Can you see the one she's got of us when we were babies?'

'It's too small to see from here.'

'Go and have a look.'

James tucked the phone against his ear with his shoulder and got up, carefully adjusting the hold he had on the sleeping baby. He walked towards the bookshelf. He knew the picture Eddie was talking about, he just hadn't looked at it for a long time. The photo had been taken in Dundee, where the three Grisham boys and their big sister Ella had grown up. The triplets were about four or five months old at that point, lying in a row on the floor, grinning up at the camera. And each of the triplets had spikes of dark hair going in every direction.

If Ivy had been transported back in time to lie on the floor with the three boys, she would have been a perfect match.

The thought was enough to give James a very strange sensation deep inside his chest. A sensation he couldn't identify exactly, but it felt familiar—like an echo of how he felt when he spoke to or saw one of his brothers when they'd been out of touch for a while?

A feeling of *connection*?

No… James didn't want to feel like this. He needed to keep his doctor's hat on and view this situation from a distance that wasn't going to be influenced by emotion. Lives could be at stake, otherwise.

His life—as he knew it?

Eddie's voice broke the silence and his tone was sombre. 'Did she get left on your doorstep? With a note on the basket?'

'Nothing that dramatic.' James was watching the way Ivy was scrunching up her face. Was she about to wake up and start crying again? He'd been up with her for hours now, trying to let Sarah get as much sleep as possible. 'Well… actually, it was kind of that dramatic. The woman who brought her here collapsed with a hypoglycaemic episode. I had to give her a dextrose infusion.'

'She's diabetic?'

'Type one.'

'And she's driving around with a baby?'

'It's not her fault.' James wasn't sure why he felt such a strong desire to defend Sarah, but there it was. 'She normally has very good control. She's got a viral infection. Probably flu. That's why I can't come for that hike today. I need to make sure she's okay and look after Ivy.'

'And what then…?'

James could feel how damp Ivy's bottom was against his arm. He could also feel her whole body starting to move. He let his breath out in a sigh. 'I don't know. I hadn't been thinking any further than getting through the night, to be fair. And talking to you, seeing as you're the only family member currently on this side of the planet.'

'Do you need us to come over?'

Us… Eddie was part of a couple now. He and Jodie were as much in love as it was possible to be and James was very happy for his brother. Thrilled even, but he wasn't sure that their company would make this any easier.

'I think I need to talk to Sarah properly, first. She hasn't explained exactly why she's here, other than to tell me that she's the baby's guardian and I'm the father. It could be that there are relatives—grandparents, maybe—that are planning to get involved and raise the kid. Or she might be planning to put her up for adoption or something and needs my consent?'

'How would you feel about that?'

'I don't know.'

Okay…that wasn't entirely honest. He'd probably feel relieved, wouldn't he? Not about adoption to unknown strangers, but a stable family unit of grandparents and possibly extended family was a very different proposition. Even having someone here who wasn't related but had been prepared to take on legal responsibility for Ivy was a relief.

'Hmm.' Eddie didn't sound convinced either. 'We're here if you need us.'

'I know. Thanks…'

'Are you going to tell Ella next?'

'No. I don't even know where she and Logan are right now.' The reason James was here, housesitting for his sister, was because she and her husband were taking a long overdue honeymoon, exploring New Zealand in a camper van.

'They're in the South Island, I believe. Around Queenstown. Last I heard, they were going to do some Lord of the Rings tour. They're having a ball.'

'Good for them. Maybe don't tell her about this yet. Or Mick.'

'He's not having a ball.' Eddie was shaking his head.

'It's not another UTI, is it? Or something worse?'

James's heart was sinking. The third triplet, Mick, had been injured badly enough in a hang-gliding accident a few months ago to be facing the rest of his life in a wheelchair. The reason that New Zealand had been chosen as a honeymoon destination by Ella and Logan had been partly because it had enabled them to travel with Mick and take him to a world-renowned rehabilitation centre there.

'No, nothing like that,' Eddie reassured him. 'But you know that cute blonde who got assigned as his physiotherapist?'

'I think her name's Riley.'

'Yeah…well, he had a row with her yesterday. She told him if he wasn't going to stop feeling so sorry for himself she wasn't going to be able to keep working with him.'

'Really? Doesn't sound very professional. She must be used to people who find it hard to come to terms with a spinal injury after leading such an active life.'

Ivy let out a whimper that made it sound like she also disapproved of this Riley's approach.

'Sounds like she gave him chapter and verse about some of the tetraplegic patients she's worked with and how thankful they would be to have the potential Mick's got to have an amazing quality of life. How the only thing that's holding him back right now is his attitude.'

'How do you know all this?'

'Spoke to him last night. He wanted to know if I agreed with her.'

'You didn't say yes, did you?'

'I kind of did. I said we'd all been worried about his state of mind since the accident. That was why we'd come up with the plan to send him to a rehab centre that looked as if it might help.'

'What did he say?'

'He's obviously thinking hard about it all. He said he was sorry for everything he's put us through. I told him to apologise to Riley. We'll have to wait and see what happens next, I guess.'

'I've got to go,' James warned. 'Things are going to get noisy around here any second now. They don't smell so great either. I think I've got a pair of pants that need changing.'

'I'll bet you have.' Eddie was grinning again. 'And you might want to change Ivy's too. Talk to you later, bro. Good luck!'

* * *

Feathers…

Was that the secret?

Maybe it was some other natural fibre, like wool, that was making this bed so comfortable it felt like a nest that Sarah never wanted to crawl out of. The duvet was fluffy and light and there seemed to be a soft topper on the mattress. The fat, squashy pillows had moulded themselves so well around her head that she couldn't quite tell where her face ended and the pillow began.

But something had not only woken her up but was nagging her to move.

Oh, yeah…that quiet but insistent ringtone on her mobile phone was an alarm that her blood sugar levels needed attention.

The air felt cold on her bare arm as she reached for the device on the bedside table and her shoulder hurt. So did her elbow. Even the joints in her hand were aching and it was quite hard to open her eyes far enough to peer at the screen of her phone.

She had expected to see that her blood glucose levels had gone up higher than an acceptable level, given that she felt as if she'd been asleep for days but, weirdly, it was a low level that had triggered this alarm. The level wasn't low enough for her to be in danger of losing consciousness, however. Or to explain the kind of brain fog that was bordering on major confusion. Had she not eaten enough yesterday? Or given herself an incorrect dose of insulin?

The small tube of fast-acting, chewy glucose tablets she could see directly in her line of vision was familiar enough but Sarah couldn't remember putting them on this table. Or pouring the glass of fruit juice that was beside them, along with a small blister pack of paracetamol capsules.

She'd never actually *seen* this particular table before, in fact.

Sarah realised how much her head was aching as she tried to make sense of odd impressions that were the last things she could remember.

Being helped up a set of stairs by a man with strong hands and a reassuring voice. A man who looked like every woman's tall, dark and handsome fantasy. Sarah could almost hear an echo of his voice as she pushed herself up onto one elbow to reach for the glass of juice. She needed sugar and this liquid form would work fast and disperse the remnants of what could be a confusing dream. A couple of those anti-inflammatories seemed like a good idea too, with so much of her body aching.

It was as she swallowed the capsules that Sarah realised it wasn't simply an echo she was hearing of that voice. Snatches of words were floating upstairs.

'...we'd all been worried...since the accident...'

What accident?

Her brain was clearing. Sarah could remember the long car drive. She could also hear something other than the soft tones of this man's voice. A sound that cut straight into her heart.

Ivy...

And she was crying.

Sarah pushed back the fluffy duvet. Her legs were as bare as her arms but her jeans were draped over the end of the bed, along with the woollen jumper she'd been wearing over her tee shirt yesterday. She wasn't about to waste any brain power trying to remember getting undressed, even though the sight of her abandoned bra was a little concerning. She didn't bother putting it back on and just pulled her jumper over the tee shirt she'd been sleeping in. She pulled on her jeans but left her boots and socks on the floor, only grabbing her phone as she made her way out of the room.

This was urgent.

The stone steps felt cold beneath her bare feet but there was a fire blazing in the living area below and, suddenly, Sarah could remember everything. This man—James Grisham. Having a hypo that had been serious enough to be dangerous, not only to herself but to the precious baby she had promised to protect and cherish.

Worst of all, Sarah realised that it had been James who had helped her up to that bed last night.

Had he taken her bra off…?

Oh…dear Lord. Sarah had to pause at the foot of the stairs, still clutching the banister rail. Her cheeks felt as if they were on fire.

'Hey…' James looked up from where he was kneeling on the floor, grappling with changing Ivy's nappy. 'I'm not sure you should be out of bed. You look like you're still running a bit of a fever.'

'I'm fine.' The warmth of the fire was welcome as Sarah went closer. 'You've got that nappy on back to front,' she told him. 'It's a lot easier to make the sticky tabs work if they're the other way round.'

'Oh… Maybe that's what Ivy was trying to tell me.'

The look that might have been relief on Ivy's face was enough to bring a lump to Sarah's throat. The bond she had formed with this tiny person in just a matter of weeks was astonishingly powerful. Ivy had even stopped crying, having spotted the face she was most familiar with.

'Here…let me.' Sarah crouched beside James,

lifted Ivy's bottom by holding both her feet in one hand and turned the disposable nappy. Then she fastened it and poked the baby's feet into the legs of her onesie. Ivy was protesting again by the time she was snapping the stud buttons shut and the sound made Sarah feel appallingly guilty about having left her in someone else's care.

'Has she had some formula?' Her tone came out more sharply than she had expected. 'Has she had any sleep?' She reached to pick Ivy up. 'Do you even know anything about looking after babies?'

'She's still alive,' James pointed out calmly. 'So I think I know enough. Yes, she's had some sleep. More than me. And yes, she's also had some formula. I found the can in your bag. Luckily, I know how to read so it wasn't too difficult to follow the instructions on the label.'

Sarah winced, cuddling Ivy a little closer. 'Sorry…' She looked up, expecting to find an angry man looking back but, if anything, James was looking as if he was on the verge of smiling at her. 'Thank you for looking after her. And me…'

'How are you feeling?'

'A bit rubbish. Kind of achy.'

'How's your BGL?'

'My alarm went off to let me know it was low. Did I give myself any insulin last night?'

'No. I've been on the couch all night. I would have noticed if you'd gone past me in the direction of the fridge, which is where I've put your insulin. Your levels were good after the dextrose infusion and that sandwich you finally finished. You looked like you fell asleep as soon as your head hit the pillow but I knew you'd applied a new continuous monitor so I didn't think I needed to disturb you to poke your finger overnight.'

'But you left the supplies there, like the juice and glucose tabs?'

James nodded. 'You'll need some food too, if you're low. We also need to talk, but we're not going to do that until I'm satisfied that you're feeling well enough.'

'I've got some muesli bars in my bag.'

'I was thinking more along the lines of some hot, buttered toast.'

Oh...comfort food... Perhaps she wasn't feeling quite so bad, after all.

'I'd like that,' Sarah admitted. 'But I can make it if you tell me where the kitchen is.'

James only lifted a single eyebrow but she could imagine what he was looking at. A flushed and probably totally dishevelled woman with bed hair and only half her clothes on, sitting on the floor like a deflated balloon with a still grizzly baby in her arms. Talk about seeing someone at their worst—or had that been when she'd keeled over in front of him last night? Maybe he could even read her mind right now and see that she was wondering how she was going to get to her feet without her knees giving way or dropping Ivy as she tried to keep her balance, let alone making it as far as a kitchen?

'Let's see if you can make it to the couch first,' was all he said. He put a hand under her elbow to help her up, and when she gratefully sank onto the corner of the couch closest to the fire he draped a soft mohair blanket over her legs. 'Don't move,' he ordered. 'I'll be back with some toast and a cup of tea. Did you take any of that paracetamol I left upstairs?'

'Yes.'

'Good. It should bring your temperature down and make you feel better soon. What would you like on your toast? Jam?' A corner of his mouth twitched. 'Cheese?'

'Um…would you have any peanut butter?'

'I'm sure there'll be some somewhere. Stand by…'

Sarah watched him disappear through the gap on the other side of the fireplace and found herself struggling to swallow past the lump that had reappeared in her throat.

Looking the way he did was more than enough

to explain why Karly had been attracted enough to James to have that fateful one-night stand.

Did he have to be so damned *nice* as well?

Sarah had thought the man she'd been coming to confront would be only too happy to sign away an inconvenient problem that his playboy lifestyle had produced. Now, she was beginning to wonder if she should have followed her instincts and stayed as far away from him as possible. She could have had, ooh…maybe fifteen years before Ivy got curious enough about her biological father to want to do anything about it.

But, for Sarah, it would have been difficult to ignore that black cloud in the distance. Giving both herself and Ivy the security of certainty had been the driving force to come here when the risk that the outcome wouldn't be what she wanted had seemed extremely small. Like that blonde woman hanging off his arm last night, Sarah had been sure she knew exactly what James Grisham was like and she'd been so confident that even the idea of fatherhood would have him running for the hills.

But then she'd met him.

She was almost certain that Karly hadn't told her the whole truth.

And that black cloud of uncertainty felt even more threatening now. Hovering right over her head, in fact. Ivy's father might be a lot nicer than she'd imagined but that was actually ringing alarm bells. Of course he was charming—that was the modus operandi for playboys, wasn't it? And men who were driven by their sex lives were at the completely opposite end of the spectrum to the kind of men Sarah admired. They were totally unsuitable, not only as life partners but very likely as an ideal father figure.

But she had to face facts. And obey rules, for that matter. Like promises, they were something else that Sarah had never broken in her life. James—in conjunction with the UK's legal system—had the power to interfere with the future Sarah had promised Karly she would provide for Ivy.

Destroy it, even?

No. She wasn't going to let that happen.

She might not be firing on all cylinders, physically or emotionally, but she knew her rights as Ivy's legal guardian and she was more than ready to fight for them, if that was what it was going to take. Because this was for Karly. And Ivy. And for herself. Sarah might be at the bottom of that list but that didn't make it any less imperative.

She had a promise to keep.

CHAPTER FOUR

JAMES WAS WATCHING her like a hawk.

The plate of peanut butter toast and the mug of tea was waiting on the coffee table in front of the couch while Sarah took a finger prick blood glucose reading to confirm the information she was receiving from her device, calculated the carbs in the breakfast she was planning to eat and dialled up the amount of the rapid-acting insulin she needed to take.

She didn't mind that he was watching her. It was making her feel a little self-conscious, but it wasn't as if it was male attention on her body due to any sexual interest. James was a doctor. He'd already had to pull her back from a hypoglycaemic episode so he had a professional interest in what was going on, that was all. He confirmed that when he spoke.

'Just out of interest, why do you go to all the trouble of the calculations you need to make and having to do multiple injections during the day instead of using an automatic insulin pump?'

'It's not like I have anything against technology,' Sarah told him. 'I love my continuous glucose monitor. Total game-changer. I've got an app to work out the insulin to carb ratio if it's food I'm not familiar with, but something like toast is easy.'

'Does managing it yourself give better control?'

'For me, yes. And I don't have the stress of pump failures, skin reactions or working around things like having a shower. I've given pumps a good go over the years too, but I always go back to this.'

It had become even more important to know that she had an almost foolproof system when she'd had the stress of learning how to care for a newborn baby. Sarah pulled up her jumper and tee shirt just enough to expose a small patch of her abdomen, pressed the tiny needle against the skin she pinched together and then pushed the button to deliver the dose.

'I get the impression you like having complete control in your life.' James was nodding. 'You seem to plan ahead and be very organised. It was very easy to find anything I needed for Ivy—and you—in that bag. The luggage pods are even labelled.'

Was he criticising her? Not everybody had the luxury of letting life flow around them and choosing any pleasurable distractions that they had the time and inclination to pursue. It was no wonder her tone was a little defensive as she responded.

'I got diagnosed with type one diabetes when I was only twelve.' She put the cap back onto her insulin pen with a decisive click. 'My grandma was really nervous about anything to do with needles so I had to learn how to manage it myself from day one. I use a long-acting insulin for background control and a rapid-acting one to cope with meals or exercise.' She lifted her chin. 'I've had twenty-two years of practice, so it's something I'm really good at, but I'll be even more careful now after last night's wakeup call.'

They both glanced towards Ivy. Sarah had tucked her into her car seat cocoon when she'd fallen asleep while James was making breakfast and she could expect her to sleep for at least ninety minutes at this time of day.

Time enough to enjoy the warmth of her own cocoon on this couch. And the toast. Sarah was surprised how good it tasted.

'I'm feeling a lot better,' she announced, between bites. 'It was probably just some twenty-four-hour bug.'

'Good to hear,' James said, but his tone held a note of caution. 'But you should rest up today.

You could go back to bed. Or stay on the couch. I can help with Ivy—I've got a day off today.'

There was something else in his tone that felt like a warning. Did he want to keep watching her to make sure she was capable of looking after a defenceless infant? Yeah…his next words made her realise her instinct was correct.

'When was the last time you had a hypo that caused you to lose consciousness? Does it always come on without any warning like that? I'm used to people being aggro or confused or getting dizzy or nauseated and so on.'

'It hasn't happened for years. And it won't happen again. I've never left my phone behind before. It was just a combination of the long drive and being sick and…and I was kind of stressed because Ivy was crying and then you arrived back suddenly. It wasn't part of the plan that you wouldn't be at home when I got here.'

James lifted an eyebrow. 'Do your plans generally work out perfectly?'

Sarah just looked at him. 'If I could control life that well, I wouldn't be here, would I? Ivy would still have her mother. And I would still have my best friend who was the closest thing I'll ever have to a sister. The only family I had left, actually.'

James got up to put a log on the fire. 'Sorry…

I don't know why I said that. Maybe because I had the feeling that you can get everything else in your life under rather impressive control.'

Sarah had lost her appetite for the toast now but she needed to keep eating to make sure her blood sugar didn't drop too far. She chased the bite down with a mouthful of tea. She wasn't offended by the idea that she gave people that impression.

'Karly used to call me a control freak,' she conceded. 'I was the organised one. I stuck to the rules. That might have been why she didn't even tell me she was pregnant until she was into her second trimester. And why she told me what she did about your reaction. She knew it would be enough to...' Her words trailed into silence.

'Enough to what?' James prompted.

'To put you right out of the picture as far as I was concerned,' Sarah admitted. 'Karly knew that I don't have time for men who aren't completely reliable. Dependable *and* careful. And kind...'

'How's that working out for you?' James sounded curious rather than nosy. 'I seem to remember you saying that it's just you and Ivy?'

Fair call. Sarah forced a smile. 'I'm single,' she agreed, tightly. 'But, on the plus side, that means there's nothing to stop me caring for Ivy. There are no other relatives on Karly's side.'

She could feel James staring at her and avoided meeting his gaze. 'I've also taken six months off work. Karly and I both thought it was the best idea.'

'And Karly has legally appointed you to be Ivy's guardian, yes?'

'Yes. It's called a testamentary guardianship. It confers parental responsibility and grants the ability to have a say in any important decisions in Ivy's long-term care and upbringing.'

It didn't mean that she had an automatic entitlement to have Ivy living with her if there was a dispute, but there was no need to tell James that yet, was there?

'What Karly really wanted was for me to formally adopt Ivy.' Sarah took a deep breath. 'So that I can be her *real* mum.'

'And that's what you want to do?'

'Yes…' Sarah not only caught James's gaze this time, she held it. 'Oh…*yes…*'

He didn't break the eye contact. 'But if I'm her biological father and you're not even genetically related to Ivy, how does that work?'

'All you have to do is sign the consent papers Karly's solicitor gave me.'

He still hadn't looked away. And Sarah couldn't. She might have rehearsed what she intended to say to Ivy's father when she found him but she hadn't bargained on someone looking at her like this.

As if what she was doing was somehow very, very wrong?

Wow…

He'd been presented with an unexpected baby and now it was going to be whisked out of his life?

No…not 'it'. Ivy was a 'she'.

A real person.

He watched Sarah, who was eating the rest of her piece of toast with an expression that suggested it was purely medicinal. James allowed himself several deep breaths before he said anything else and even then he had to be careful to keep his tone neutral.

'So…' he said, finally. 'I sign your papers and what then? I know I have a daughter but I never see her again? She grows up thinking that her father wasn't even interested in her?'

Sarah was biting her lip, looking uncomfortable.

'Why did Karly even make a witnessed statement about me being Ivy's father?'

'She said it was kind of an insurance policy. In case Ivy needed something like a bone marrow transplant or a kidney donation.'

A shiver ran down his spine. 'Have they picked up a health issue with Ivy?'

'No…she's fine. I think she was just imagining things that might go wrong in the future.' Sarah shook her head, as if dismissing his concern. 'And she'll know who you are. We can stay in contact with photos and video calls and things. You can visit any time you want to. I can bring her up to Scotland to visit you.' She was offering him a tentative smile. 'I know the way, now.'

Even a small smile changed Sarah's face from being one that he wouldn't have noticed particularly if she'd walked past him in the street, but James stamped on the thought that she was more attractive than he'd realised.

'Where is it that you live?' he asked.

'Leeds.'

'And do you work?'

'Yes. I'm a nurse. So was Karly. We did our training together and then looked for jobs at the same hospital so we could share a flat. We ended up in the same department in the end because we both loved Emergency so much. We both graduated as Emergency nurse practitioners about a year ago.'

James blinked. A nurse practitioner qualification was the highest rank for nurses. It gave them the scope of practice to diagnose and treat minor injuries and discharge patients without them having to wait to be seen by a doctor.

'To be honest, though,' Sarah continued, 'I prefer to be part of a team and the Resus room is my absolute favourite place to work. After we did a MIMMS course I even wondered if I should switch to being a paramedic.'

'You've done MIMMS—Major Incident Medical Management and Support?' James was impressed. 'So did I, when I was working with a HEMS unit for a couple of years.'

'I'm part of a group. We meet once a month to do a tabletop exercise in planning and management as a refresher and take turns inventing the simulated emergency situations. It's my favourite night out.' Sarah's smile was wry. 'Or it used to be, anyway.' It looked as though she was consigning that part of her life to the past. 'I was supposed to have gone to that conference in Paris where you met Karly,' she added. 'The only reason I didn't was because my grandmother was dying. She'd been sick for a long time.'

James had been drawn to that conference because of its focus on disaster management. Emergency medicine was his own passion and the drama of working in a resuscitation area made it his favourite place to be as well. Right now, he was feeling a connection that he wasn't sure he wanted to have with Sarah Harrison.

'But you've taken time off work.'

She nodded. 'With my savings I can cover at least six months.'

'And after that?'

'I've got a great job I can go back to. There's also a good creche near the hospital that I can get Ivy into.'

'You've got it all planned, then.'

'Karly and I spent the last weeks of her life talking about it so…yeah…'

It felt as if Sarah was avoiding meeting his gaze now. Shutting him out?

'What would happen if I didn't sign those papers?'

Her gaze flicked up. Her face tightened. 'I'd still be Ivy's guardian. I'll still look after her. And protect her.'

'What if I want to look after her?' James wasn't sure if he was playing devil's advocate or whether he needed to hear the words aloud to see if they might be true. 'What if I want her to live with me? The hospital where I work—The Queen Mother's—has an excellent creche on site, I believe.'

He couldn't miss the unmistakable flash of fear in Sarah's eyes and James felt an urge to tell her everything was going to be okay, because there was something about those wide eyes in that pale face underneath hair that looked as if it hadn't seen a hairbrush in a very long time that was pulling at his heartstrings. Pushing buttons in a part of him that he'd finally gained much better control of as an adult. The part that made it impossible not to care more about the feelings of the people he loved than his own.

But he couldn't afford to let anything emotional run rampant right now. And he couldn't assure Sarah that this was all going to have a happy ending, could he? His world had been turned so abruptly upside down that James wasn't sure what was going to happen in the next five minutes, let alone the next five years.

'It would have to go to court,' Sarah said quietly. 'A judge would make a decision about what should happen in Ivy's best interests.'

She was staring at him.

He was staring back at her.

And then a small squeak from the direction of the car seat made them both turn their head sharply. Ivy was awake again.

Not crying, though. She was moving her arms. Holding them up as if she wanted Sarah to pick her up. Or did she want to check that her hands were still attached to the end of them? James found himself smiling at the notion as he looked at those tiny hands and all those perfect little fingers.

Ivy seemed to be looking straight up at Sarah

but James had a very clear view of her face so he could see the moment the baby's lips began to curve.

He could hear Sarah's gasp. 'Oh…are you smiling, Ivy?' Sarah was blinking as if she was close to shedding a tear as she slid a graze of eye contact in James's direction to see if he could see what she was seeing. 'It's her first smile…'

Ivy was getting the hang of it quite fast in that case, James thought. Both sides of that miniature mouth were curving up and there were even little crinkles around her eyes. And when she opened her mouth she looked like she was the happiest baby on earth. She even made a sound—a delicious little gurgle—and it was then that James could feel something melting inside him.

His heart, perhaps?

'I can't do it,' he heard himself saying.

'Do what?' Sarah's head swerved towards him.

'I can't sign those papers. I can't let you just take Ivy away from me.'

If this was a chess game, James had just fired the warning shot of announcing 'check'.

It was not as final as a 'checkmate' where Sarah would have no choice but to concede total defeat but it was still an undeniable shock that she tried to hide by sliding off the couch and kneeling in front of the car seat to smile back at Ivy.

She couldn't deny, however, that she could feel a smidge of what could only be relief.

Because James was, unless proved otherwise, Ivy's father and it hadn't felt right suggesting that he sign away his responsibilities as a parent. It wasn't simply that he had the right to be a part of Ivy's life. It was because Sarah had seen the look on his face when Ivy had bestowed her first ever smile on the world and…

…and it meant something.

Something huge enough to have made her heart hurt. Because Sarah—and Karly, for that matter—had known what it was like to grow up without having a mum or dad. Sarah had been so much luckier than Karly, having a doting grandmother whom she adored, who had been only too willing to step into the gap left when her parents had both been killed in a dreadful car crash. But, even though she'd been too young to really remember them, she'd still felt the hole in her life from not having what she'd always thought of as a 'real' family.

That had been the connection that had bound her and Karly together so tightly. That was the reason why Sarah hadn't hesitated in her promise to look after Ivy for the rest of her life. Now it was the reason that, no matter how difficult this might become, she had to accept that James was also going to be part of her life. *Their* lives? That was possibly the best-case scenario Sarah could hope for, here. If it went to court, who was to say that a judge wouldn't decide that Ivy would be better off living with her father than simply with a friend of her mother's?

Sarah swallowed hard. Her voice was no more than a whisper as she looked up at James. 'I'm not going to walk away from the promise I made to Karly. I *can't*… I was there when Ivy was born. I was the first person to hold her. I didn't just promise Karly, I promised Ivy—even if I didn't say it out loud in those first minutes. I'm her guardian.' She managed to not let a wobble creep into her voice. 'Or are you planning to fight that?'

She couldn't stop the tears that were sneaking into her eyes. This renewed threat of tears was very different to the joyful reaction to Ivy's first smile she had just blinked back. Because this meant so much and because she was still feeling unwell enough that the prospect of having to fight for it was almost overwhelming.

Because part of her believed James could win that battle and another part wanted him to, so that Ivy would have a father who loved her enough to be prepared to fight for her.

Like she'd never had…?

* * *

Oh…*no*…

Tears were something that had the ability to leak past any protective barriers James might have developed over so many years of dealing with people in situations that were terrifying or painful or tragic.

Women's tears were always that much harder.

Especially from strong, courageous women who were determined to protect any children in their care.

Like Sarah.

Like his mother had been…

The whole family had been devastated when the struggle to survive a terminal diagnosis began for Colleen Grisham, but for James it was as if he could feel the weight of everyone else's fear and grief on top of his own. Ella had been away at university already, training to become a nurse, but she'd come home as often as she could because the triplets were only teenagers and their father was barely coping with the practicalities, let alone the emotions of such a difficult time. It was James who'd learned to appear strong enough to offer comfort to his mum, his dad and his brothers. Who'd learned to bottle up his own tears and be so aware of the first sign of them in anyone else.

Who'd known that the best way to protect

himself in the future was not to add anyone else into that close circle he had around him—the people he loved as much as life itself.

Sarah might be safely miles away from that circle but it still tore his heart a little to see the way her eyes were sparkling with the extra moisture that was gathering in them. Any moment now, a drop would roll down her face and he'd want to put his arms around her and hold her close.

He had to try and get control of this—for both their sakes.

'*No*,' he said emphatically. 'That's not what I mean at all.'

Ivy was squeaking again and Sarah reached to pick her up but James saw the way she hesitated for a heartbeat, closing her eyes as if she needed to gather strength.

'Here…' He moved to crouch on the floor beside her. 'Let me…'

He didn't wait for a response, sliding his hands underneath the baby to support her head and her body as he lifted her and then got to his feet. 'I meant it when I said you needed to rest today, Sarah. If you don't, you're not going to get better quickly and…and Ivy needs you.'

Her eyes were wide and the tears seemed to have magically evaporated. There was something that looked like hope in them as he said that and it made James feel good.

As good as it might have felt to comfort Sarah with a hug?

She was pushing herself upright and went back to sit on the couch. She looked like she would much prefer to lie down but she wasn't going to. Not yet.

'What *did* you mean, then?' she asked. 'You're hardly in a position to raise Ivy by yourself, are you?'

'I wouldn't be by myself.' Ivy seemed to be enjoying being held and was quietly gazing up at the man holding her, so James walked over to the bookshelf and picked up the photo Eddie had reminded him about. He handed it to Sarah by way of underlining his statement.

Her jaw dropped. 'Is one of those babies you?'

'Aye.'

'But there's three of you.'

He smiled at her. 'There generally is with triplets.'

Sarah didn't see the smile because her gaze was still fixed on the photo, but Ivy did and she smiled right back at him.

'Your *hair*...' Sarah whispered.

'I know, right?' James had no right to feel this proud of something he had no control over. 'The Grisham genes are clearly strong.

'We've got an older sister too. Ella. Well, she's a half-sister because our dad came along years after her own dad died. Mum and Dad really wanted a baby but it wasn't working so they used IVF and, as they always told people, it worked a bit too well. We're not identical triplets but we may as well be. We're a tight unit and, thanks to Mick's accident and Eddie falling in love with Jodie, it looks like we're all going to be living close to each other.' He took a deep breath. 'Bottom line is that I've got a pretty good support network.'

'A whole family,' Sarah agreed quietly, putting the photo down on the coffee table.

James nodded. 'One that you could also be a part of. You're involved too and nobody's going to shut you out. I can promise you that.'

'But I don't live here.'

'I didn't either until there was something important enough to make it the best option.' James wasn't going to say anything more. There were too many threads to untangle to get distracted by logistics.

'What if Ivy was *your* baby?' he asked quietly. 'You would want her to know her father, wouldn't you?'

'Yes...'

'You'd want to share the parenthood if it could

work, wouldn't you? To share the costs? The decisions? The worry…?'

He just let those threads float in the air too.

'What I'm saying is that we're both involved and we need to make a plan around that. But we also need to get to know each other. You, me *and* Ivy.'

Ivy started whimpering as if she knew she was being talked about.

'Is it time for her to have another feed?' James asked. 'I can make up some formula.'

'When did you last feed her?'

'I'm not sure. Maybe five-thirty a.m.? Ish…?'

'And she had a nappy change about an hour later but she didn't sleep as long as usual…' Sarah was frowning as she looked at her watch. 'Her schedule is all over the place. She should have slept for a few hours. I hope she hasn't caught whatever bug I've got.'

'She's not running a temperature. I think she needs a sleep—like you do. Why don't I take her out for a while? There's some paperwork I'd like to pick up from my office at the hospital, seeing as I'm going to have a day at home, and I'm sure there are a few supplies we're going to need for Ivy.'

'But…we need to talk.'

'There's plenty of time for that. You can stay

here. Get over this bug. There's no need for you to rush back to Leeds, is there?'

'I've got a GP appointment booked for Ivy to have her eight-week vaccinations but that's not till next week so I guess there's nothing urgent...' But Sarah sounded hesitant.

'Have a sleep. A shower, if you feel like it. There's a stack of clean towels in the bathroom upstairs and plenty of shampoo and so on. Help yourself to anything you want to eat or drink too. I'll take the bag with the formula and nappies and everything and I'll be back in a few hours.'

Her jaw had dropped. 'On a motorbike? Are you *kidding*?'

'My sister's car is in the garage. I'm using it sometimes to keep the battery charged.'

'Does it have safety belts in the back? Ivy's car seat has to be in the back. Rear-facing. In the centre seat because, statistically, that's the safest place—furthest away from any potential impact.'

'I could always drive your car.'

James gave her his best smile. Not that it was a conscious decision, like giving someone a *Trust me, I'm a doctor* smile or an *It'll be worth it, I promise* kind of smile. This was a *real* smile. One of genuine appreciation. An offer of friendship?

'I feel like I know you already,' he added.

'And I'm willing to bet you've chosen the safest model out there. You know you can trust me to keep Ivy safe.' James was serious now. 'And I know you're perfectly capable of looking after yourself, Sarah, but I'll do whatever I can to keep you safe as well. You're the closest thing Ivy has to a mother and she needs you. Don't you, Ivy?'

He was rocking the baby as he looked down to include her in the conversation, partly because he wanted to give Sarah a moment to think about what he was offering. Would she trust him enough to give herself the chance to close her eyes and escape for a while from what could very well be an impossible emotional overload.

And then James looked up and caught her gaze. '*I* need you,' he added softly. 'We're in this together, okay?'

Sarah didn't say anything.

But when she finally nodded slowly it felt like a win. As if they had taken the first steps in the right direction, even though neither of them had a map for this journey they were both on.

Oh…that *smile*…

The one she'd felt all the way down to her toes.

She was feeling it again when she was standing under the hot rain of an excellent shower hours later. Or was she just feeling so much better? And grateful for the chance to rest? Sarah hadn't had such a deep sleep in weeks. Months, even, because she had been poised for any change in Karly's condition and then to attend to any needs of a newborn baby.

The thought that she'd trusted a total stranger enough to let him take Ivy away to allow herself to get the kind of rest her body was desperate for was unbelievable but, weirdly, Sarah only had to remember that smile to keep her anxiety at bay. Or perhaps she was remembering that he had not only saved her life, he hadn't judged her to be an unfit mother for Ivy in the wake of that incident.

He'd even said that she was the closest thing to an actual mother that Ivy had and that she was needed, and that had been the most affirming thing anybody had said to her in these last, traumatic weeks when her life had altered beyond recognition.

He'd said *he* needed her too, and somehow, while she'd been sleeping, she'd begun to process it. Despite the opinion of this man that had been so firmly embedded in her head before she'd met him and was still lingering at the back of her mind, everything James had said was resonating on a level that was undeniably attractive. His words were creating thoughts that had the potential to slip into any gaps in the plans she'd been making for her own and Ivy's future.

They could smooth the rough patches of how hard Sarah knew it was going to be sometimes as a single parent, like the worries about money or choosing the right school or being terrified of a sudden high fever. How much better would it be to have someone else to share the weight of responsibility of raising a child—like she and Karly had been planning to do before they knew how sick Karly was.

There was a much more positive side to this coin too. It wasn't simply the relief of being able to discuss the pros and cons of big decisions or sharing any struggles. It would mean having someone else who was just as invested in celebrating the special things like first steps or words or delighted to stick a crayon scribble that was supposed to be a person onto the fridge with a magnet.

And there was something so much bigger than any of this that was on offer. James Grisham had a whole family. Confirmation by way of a DNA test would be needed, of course, to make everything certain and legal but it did appear that Ivy was genetically linked to the Grishams and that meant that even in the innermost circle there were aunts and uncles, along with her father, available to offer love and care and the anchor of home for the rest of her life.

James was even suggesting that Sarah could be a part of it because of her connection to Ivy.

Sarah's tears were mingling with the water from the shower as she tilted her head back. She wasn't going to rush into anything unless she knew it could be trusted a thousand percent but…but wasn't this exactly what Karly would have dreamed of for her baby?

To have an entire family just appear out of nowhere?

For Ivy, it was like winning a lottery that you couldn't even buy a ticket for.

CHAPTER FIVE

IT HAD BEEN beyond busy all day.

The Accident and Emergency department in Aberdeen's Queen Mother's Hospital had been unusually hectic during this weekend shift that James Grisham had been rostered on for. He'd been thrown into the deep end as soon as he'd changed into his scrubs, draped his lanyard and stethoscope around his neck and clipped his pager to his pocket—walking into the department at the same moment a middle-aged patient under CPR was being brought in from the ambulance bay.

That the resuscitation attempt was successful made it one of those great days to be fighting life or death battles but there'd be no time for anyone to do anything more than smile at each other and say something like 'Well done', or 'Good job, wasn't it?' James had barely stopped moving since that first case, with his duties including triaging the patients coming in by ambulance so that he could choose the appropriate areas for them to go to. Resuscitation was for the most critically ill patients, Majors for serious cases and Minors for anything that could wait for a while if necessary.

The ones coming in by ambulance tended to be the time critical injuries and medical emergencies, like the man whose heart had stopped, apparently due to an arrhythmia. James had later dealt with two people with chest pain and evolving heart attacks, a major stroke, trauma from a cyclist being hit by a car, a bowel obstruction, three people with abdominal pain, one of whom had appendicitis and another with acute biliary colic from gallstones, respiratory infections, a couple of broken bones and—even though he was due to go off duty in about ten minutes, he was on his way to meet an ambulance which was coming in with someone who might have a chicken bone lodged in his throat.

'I can take this one.' A consultant who was covering the department until midnight caught up with James as he headed for the automatic doors that led out to the ambulance bay. 'Isn't it about time you went home?'

'I'm happy.' James waved him off. 'But I'll leave the next one for you. There's an ambulance with an ETA of two minutes with a Status One from a motorway pile-up on board, and there's more to come. You're going to be busy for a while.'

'True.' His colleague grinned at him. 'Just the way we like it.'

James threw a smile over his shoulder. A great emergency department—like this one at Queen's—could provide everything you could hope for in the huge variety of cases and severity, great facilities and colleagues to both work with and refer patients to and, for the most part today, he'd been treating people who were more than grateful for the help and reassurance they needed so badly when they were having a seriously bad day.

But how ironic was it that the chaos and challenges of this job were suddenly the familiar constants in a life that had changed irrevocably in a matter of only days? The eye of the hurricane happening in his personal life, in fact? James had known he was destined to work in emergency medicine ever since he'd been at medical school and he'd always loved his job, but over the last week, having a day like this where there was barely a moment to think about anything else, in a department he now felt completely at home in, had become even more of a happy place—a respite from the shock of having his world not just tipped upside down but shaken hard at the same time.

Not that it was an ordeal to have Sarah and Ivy still staying with him at the barn. He hadn't given her any choice but to stay that first night, and the next night she'd still felt unwell enough for it to have been the only sensible thing to do, but her decision might have also been influenced by the bit of shopping he'd done on the way home from picking up that paperwork from his office. It was just as well he had taken Sarah's roomy SUV because it had required two of the baby emporium's staff members to pack in all the supplies he'd managed to gather in a very short space of time, like a bassinet and linen, a baby bath, nappies, extra clothes and tins of formula. Oh, aye…there'd been that square of the softest fabric he'd ever felt that had a small and super cute, fluffy little lamb on one corner so that the rest of the square looked like a dress it was wearing.

Who knew that there were things like this and that they were, adorably, called 'loveys'?

Sarah obviously knew and James had a feeling that it was that smallest purchase that had sealed the deal and stopped her heading off to find somewhere else to stay with Ivy until she was well enough to head home.

She had recovered more each day and James realised that his first impressions of her determination to overcome any obstacles in her life by a mix of courage and rigid organisational skills hadn't given him the full picture by any means. She was devoted to Ivy to a degree that made James envy the friendship she must have had with Karly. She was so good at managing her diabetes that it was easy to imagine that, under normal circumstances, nobody would know about it unless she chose to tell them. She was also highly intelligent and…and great company. She and Jodie had hit it off instantly when Eddie had insisted they brought dinner round for them both the other day, and Ella and Logan had clearly liked her when they met her via the video call they'd made the day the DNA results came through and confirmed what James had already been quite sure of in his own heart.

Ivy was his daughter.

And that knowledge, along with the huge responsibility to protect this infant and the chaos of considering the future, came with a sense of wonder and pride that he'd contributed to creating this small human with the most amazing hair and smile in the entire world. Thoughts of Ivy and, by default, of Sarah were always in the back of his mind and could be tapped into at any time, but James had been an emergency physician for many years now and it was easy to shut any mental doors that kept him from being distracted from his job.

Which was why it was such a respite to be here, especially when it was hectic, and why he wasn't rushing to leave on time today. Thanks to that video call with his older sister and her husband, the clock was ticking more loudly for their return to Scotland, with Mick, in just a couple of weeks. That was on top of the already ticking clock that was counting down the days until Sarah decided it was time she went home. Depending on Ivy's cooperation, during the dinner that Sarah was cooking tonight and however long it took into the evening, it was imperative that they talked about the immediate future and how much James would be able to be present in his daughter's life.

In the meantime, however, James was going to see a young man who had been eating fried chicken for his dinner and had come straight from the fast-food restaurant to ED, convinced that he had a bone lodged in his throat. One last case for the busy shift and, more than likely, one more story he could entertain Sarah with if he wasn't quite ready to dive into the heavy conversation regarding what was going to happen next in their lives.

The beautiful barn conversion that was the home of Ella Grisham and her husband, Logan, was a joy to be staying in.

The kitchen and well-stocked pantry seemed to have been designed to cater for large family gatherings so it had been child's play to create a small dinner for two that would be forgiving if James was late getting away from the hospital. A potato gratin was in the oven, a couple of steaks were bathing in some marinade and Sarah was adding some mustard and garlic to the vinaigrette dressing she was making for a colourful, fresh salad.

And she couldn't remember the last time she had felt this good.

It was probably because she'd shaken off the last remnants of that viral illness.

Or maybe it was because it had been such a lovely day and she had gone shopping with Ivy for the groceries, explored a little bit of Aberdeen and then spent some time outside in the afternoon sunshine when they got back, watching the ducks on the pond that provided the most picturesque part of this serene rural setting.

But that didn't quite explain the fact that her sense of wellbeing had increased so noticeably since James had arrived home, and that was despite the somewhat disturbing prospect of the overdue discussion they had to have this evening about Ivy's immediate future. Sarah was finding it remarkably easy to push it out of her mind, in fact. James was clearly in no hurry to broach a serious topic, probably because he had Ivy in his arms and was holding her last bottle of milk before her bedtime. On top of that, he was busy telling her a story about his shift.

'So he's sitting there, having enough trouble swallowing to be drooling and complaining of a pain on the left side of this throat that was severe enough to prevent him turning his head to that side. No palpable mass in his neck and his lungs were clear.'

'Could you see anything?'

'No. I used a laryngoscope torch and a mouth mirror but couldn't see any trauma or swelling or even a hint of a foreign object embedded anywhere.' James leaned over the top of Ivy to put an almost empty bottle onto the kitchen table. 'I think she's full. She's almost asleep.'

'If you burp her, I'll check her nappy and then put her to bed.'

James nodded, and carefully changed the baby's position so that she was upright and well supported with one arm while he rubbed her back in circles with his other hand.

'Is this okay?' he asked.

'It's great. You can do some gentle pats as well.' Sarah wanted to hear the end of the story. 'So how did you find the chicken bone? Did you get a CT done?'

'Soft tissue, lateral neck X-ray did the trick. It

was hiding in the left tonsillar crypt, just above the hyoid bone.'

'Did you get a consult with ENT?'

'Nobody was available to do an immediate endoscopy. He was uncomfortable but it wasn't an emergency so it was suggested he could wait for an outpatient appointment tomorrow, but I didn't want to leave him like that.' James was patting Ivy's back now. 'And he didn't want to go home like that, so I suggested that I had a go myself and he was more than up for it.'

Sarah blinked. James might be new at handling babies but he wasn't lacking in confidence in other areas, was he? 'What did you do?'

'Anaesthetised his throat with Benzocaine spray, gave him some conscious sedation with Midazolam and Fentanyl and I used a video laryngoscope and then some alligator forceps to get the splinter out. Worked a treat.'

Ivy chose that moment to release an impressive burp by way of punctuation and both James and Sarah laughed aloud.

The grin that remained on James's face as he caught Sarah's gaze made it look as if he considered the burp a personal triumph.

And Sarah grinned right back at him. What woman wouldn't respond to a gorgeous man smiling at her like that? Nobody would dispute how attractive he was with that tousled dark hair, those eyes and that killer smile that held more than a smidge of mischief. His delight in the achievement of feeding and burping a baby was contagious too, especially in the wake of that rather charming doubt in his own abilities that made it clear he had none of the arrogance that such good-looking men often did have.

This was the kind of moment that all new parents must take delight in as they learned the new skills required to keep their babies happy, Sarah thought, but there were so many other layers in play here, it quickly spiralled from pleasure into trepidation. This was anything but a normal situation for new parents. She couldn't forget that James was the actual parent. That they were in the kitchen of his sister's home. That big decisions needed to be made and that, if compromise was necessary, it would very likely be Sarah who would be the one who had to concede.

And maybe she also needed to remember that James Grisham was an expert in charming women and getting what he wanted from them. She couldn't afford to fall under his spell. For Ivy's sake as much as her own.

Sarah's smile faded as she turned away to screw the lid on the jar and shake it hard to mix the olive oil and balsamic vinegar with the other ingredients.

'I'll get Ivy sorted for bed,' she said. 'It'll only take a minute to cook the steak and we'll enjoy our dinner more if she's asleep. Unless you're starving? It is getting late.'

James stood up as she walked towards him and took a now very sleepy Ivy from his arms. There was a slightly awkward moment in being this close to each other. Was James as aware as she was of the way their arms were touching? That their fingers brushed, skin to skin, as she took the weight of Ivy's head? Was that what made him clear his throat so abruptly as he stepped back?

'I know my way round a barbecue,' he said. 'Why don't I go and fire it up?'

'That would be great.'

'How do you like your steak done?'

'Just on the well-done side of medium, please.'

'I might have guessed you'd have an exact response.' James was laughing again. 'I'll do my best.'

The sound of his laughter followed Sarah as she climbed the stairs. Oddly, it didn't offend her that James thought she was as much of a control freak as Karly always had, and that was partly because it was true but also because it almost sounded as if he admired the trait rather than disapproving of it.

Or maybe it was the sound of his laughter that

felt like it was seeping into her body through her ears and trickling down to curl around her heart. She found she was smiling again herself as she took care of the baby's pre-bedtime routine.

She couldn't help herself, could she?

She liked Ivy's father.

More than she'd expected to. Way more than she should. But that was the problem with bad boys, wasn't it? They charmed you into thinking the rules didn't matter.

But they did. As much as being in control mattered. Especially for Sarah. She'd learned that long ago.

The meal was so good it seemed a shame to spoil it by opening a discussion that could rapidly become difficult, so James told her stories about growing up as one of triplet brothers.

'It was like we were a single unit. The Grisham boys. Ella called us the "Fearsome Threesome". If one of us did something, we all did it—good or bad. We never told on each other either. Ella swears it was me that stole our mother's nail scissors one time and started the haircutting incident but I'm pretty sure it was Mick.'

'Oh, no… How old were you?'

'About three. Probably old enough to know better.'

Sarah was smiling but James wanted to make

her laugh again—the way she had when Ivy had produced that magnificent belch. He wanted to see that sparkle in her eyes and feel that, just for a moment, she had forgotten the serious side of life.

Had he really thought there was nothing particularly special about her when he'd first seen her standing in his driveway that night? That she was ordinary enough to disappear into the background of some quiet place like a library or a laboratory? Maybe it was true he wouldn't have noticed her if she'd crossed his path but that would have been his loss, wouldn't it?

There was something about her that was very special indeed.

Sarah suddenly glanced up, a last mouthful on her fork poised halfway to her mouth, as if she'd somehow caught the gist of his thoughts. There was a hint more colour in her cheeks as she seemed to try and focus on what he'd just said.

'I'll bet you were a real handful as you grew up. Were you all daredevils like Mick? Are you into extreme sports like hang-gliding as well?'

'I've given it a go but I'm not as adventurous as Eddie.' James was only too happy to be redirected from wherever his thoughts had been trying to take him. 'I work in a nice, safe emergency department instead of flying into dangerous situations like he does with the air ambulance. And Mick was the one who started taking things a bit too far. I think it was a knee-jerk reaction to getting jilted but it became a habit.'

'Getting jilted?' Sarah's eyes were wide. 'You left that bit out when you were telling me about Mick's accident the other day.'

'It's years ago now. He thought he was going to become a father so he proposed to his Brazilian girlfriend, Juliana. We were all dressed up in tuxedoes, waiting at the front of the church for a bride that never turned up.'

'Why not?'

'The real father of the baby had come to find her. She was already at the airport to head back to Brazil with him by the time we'd lined up in front of the altar.'

'That's awful…'

'We did get very drunk that night,' James admitted. 'And we made a vow that none of us would go looking to get married or even caught in a permanent relationship. That we were going to live in the 'now' and make the most of our lives and our careers and the only people we needed around for ever were each other. We would celebrate the good stuff and be there for each other for any bad stuff.' He let his breath out in a sigh. 'Eddie's well and truly broken that vow now. And my wings have certainly been clipped.'

Sarah put her fork down on her plate so carefully it didn't make a sound.

'They don't have to be,' she said. 'I'm quite prepared to be Ivy's primary caregiver. It's not as if you're even in a position to be a full-time father.'

And, just like that, here they were.

About to make plans that were going to affect the rest of his life.

'Finding out I'm a father has changed my life dramatically,' James said slowly. 'But it had already changed—the moment Mick had his accident—and we all got the wake-up call that life could be a lot shorter than we might want. It's probably taken a lot longer than it should have but my brothers and I are finally growing up and settling down. Eddie's with Jodie. It sounds like Mick's turned a corner in his recovery and I won't be surprised if he gets back to a brilliant medical career—or competes in the Paralympics in the future or something. And me? I'm here for my family because that's the most important thing I have in my life other than *my* career.' James took a deep breath. 'And my family now includes my daughter. Right now, Ivy is the most important person in the world as far as I'm concerned. I'm going to find out what bureaucratic hoops I might need to jump through with the registry office to get my name officially recorded on her birth certificate and…and I really don't want you to take her back to Leeds.'

Sarah's face was completely still as she absorbed his words. 'But that's my home,' she said in a whisper. 'It's where my job is and my friends are. It's where I grew up. Where I *live*…' She shook her head. 'I can't stay here—this isn't even your house.'

'I know. I was planning to move into the apartment that Eddie's moved out of, but that's a basement flat that's not at all suitable for having a baby there even part time. I've decided I'm going to find somewhere else to rent.' James swallowed hard. 'It's too soon to think about buying anything because there are too many things still up in the air. I don't know how Mick's going to be when he gets back and my job here is just a locum position. It could be that I don't have to stay in Aberdeen for ever. I might even be up for moving to Leeds if that's what it takes to be a part of Ivy's life—who knows?'

Sarah seemed to be listening carefully. James tried not to sound as if he was pushing her. He certainly had no intention of threatening her with legalities or moral obligations to him as the biological parent. This wasn't going to work at all if they became enemies, but even if Ivy didn't exist he wouldn't want to hurt Sarah.

Because she was special.

Because he really admired her.

He really liked her. A lot...

'What I'm wondering is...if I find a big enough house, maybe you could stay longer. A few more weeks. A month? Maybe two, if it's working? We could share caring for Ivy in the same way we're doing it here? If we could take our time making the really big decisions, then isn't it more likely that they might be the best ones? For Ivy *and* for us? You don't have to give me an answer right now but would you think about it? Please...?'

He might not be pushing her but he knew that Sarah could see how important this was to him because her face—and especially her eyes— were expressive enough to reveal exactly what she was thinking. This woman might be in complete control of her life but that didn't mean she didn't feel things very deeply. He could see flashes of all sorts of emotions she was experiencing. Fear, surprise, doubt. Hope, perhaps? And something else, as her gaze finally softened, that looked like...empathy.

For him?

She was thinking this through from his point of view as well as her own and Ivy's?

Of course she was. That didn't surprise him either. On top of everything he admired about Sarah Harrison, he'd known she was compassionate and caring.

What he hadn't known was what it felt like to have her looking at *him* like this. As if she really cared. As if…they might be able to have the kind of friendship that he'd envied Karly having with Sarah so much?

Sarah was nodding slowly. 'I'll think about it,' she promised.

As she got to her feet and picked up her empty plate, James felt himself take a step closer to that friendship he'd glimpsed and…it felt surprisingly good.

Very, very different to how he'd ever felt about wanting to be close to a woman, in fact.

He was also aware of a wash of relief that Ivy wasn't going to be whisked out of his life and back to Leeds immediately. He wanted to hug Sarah. He stood up and reached for his plate but what he really wanted to do was reach for Sarah and dance around the kitchen with her.

To kiss her…?

Good grief…where the hell had that thought come from? Maybe this new feeling for the guardian of his child wasn't so different to all the other women who'd come—and gone—from his life and James felt oddly disturbed by what had to be just an automatic reaction thanks to old habits. Deplorable habits, as far as Sarah was concerned. Irresponsible playboys could be dismissed. Sex addicts should clearly be avoided at all costs.

Thank goodness he had the errant impulse under control within a heartbeat. His connection with Sarah Harrison had absolutely nothing to do with physical attraction and never would because it was based on something far more important for both of them.

Being Ivy's parents.

It was just as well Sarah had turned towards the kitchen sink.

She hadn't seen a thing.

CHAPTER SIX

'WE'LL JUST POP in for a minute.' Sarah unclipped the safety belt holding Ivy's car seat. She already had the strap of the bag, containing all the baby essentials that were now a priority in her life, over her shoulder. 'You'd like to see where your daddy works, wouldn't you, darling?'

She turned to look at the solid, square shape of Aberdeen's Queen Mother's Hospital that was modern enough for the wall of glass windows to be the most prominent feature. There were signs making it easy to find the way to Reception or Accident & Emergency, but Sarah felt as if she could see past those first main signs and through some of those countless windows to the inner workings of the hospital with its imaging departments of X-ray, MRI and Ultrasound, the operating theatres, wards and Intensive Care Units, Outpatients, Pathology—even the locker rooms, gift shops and cafeterias.

Every hospital was a world of its own but the atmosphere they had in common was always familiar and, for Sarah, it felt like home. Being a nurse was such a big part of her life. Of who she was. And she hadn't realised how much she was missing it until she walked into the reception area of Queen's and headed for the main desk to ask if they could call Emergency and see if Dr Grisham might be free for a minute or two. She was quite happy to wait.

More than happy, in fact, because it meant she could sit out here and soak in the feeling of being where she belonged. Of remembering that, while she wouldn't want to be doing anything else at this point in her life, she was more than the primary caregiver of a precious baby who had lost her real mother. One day, especially if she had support in raising Ivy, it would be possible for her to return to the job she loved so much.

Not that she got more than about sixty seconds to enjoy the bustle of a busy hospital entranceway. Wearing scrubs and an expression that didn't disguise his concern, James came striding though the opening to one of the corridors that led from the reception area.

'Sarah…what's wrong? Is it Ivy?' He crouched down in front of the car seat and tugged one of the brightly coloured toys hanging on elastic from the handle to make it dance. 'Hey… Piglet. How're you doing?'

Sarah could hear the way his breath huffed out in relief as Ivy grinned up at him.

James was smiling back at his daughter. 'She doesn't look like there's much wrong with her.'

'There isn't. Sorry… I didn't mean to get you worried by arriving unannounced. I hope we haven't interrupted something.'

'Only coffee. It's weirdly quiet in ED at the moment.' James looked up at Sarah. 'You know that "calm before the storm" kind of feeling?'

'All too well. I won't keep you. I just wanted to show you some photos of a house in Ferryhill that we went past when we drove near Duthie Park this morning. It's got a sign outside saying it's available to rent so I checked it out on the agent's website. Look…'

Sarah opened the link on her phone. 'I have no idea if it's the sort of thing you like but I noticed it because it reminds me a bit of my grandma's house where I grew up.' She showed James a picture of the lovely stone-built terraced house to rent in a leafy street, close to the lovely green park and walkways along the river. 'It's even got the same kind of wooden floors and plaster cornices.'

Sarah was looking at the image but she could feel the shift of James's glance and the way he was focusing on her. As if he'd realised instantly that this was her way of telling him that she had not only processed his suggestion and decided that she was happy to stay in Aberdeen longer but that being involved in the choice of where they would live would help her feel as if she was still, at least partly, in control of her own life.

'Come and have a coffee,' he said. 'I might even be able to take my lunch break and I'd like to see some more photos. Maybe we can call the agent and make an appointment to go and see the house.'

'Okay… I'm not in any huge hurry to get home.' Sarah turned her head. 'Which way is the cafeteria?'

'I was thinking of our staffroom,' James said. 'It'll be a lot less crowded. Would you like a quick tour of our ED on the way? It's one of the best I've worked in so I'm sure you'd appreciate the setup.'

Oh…if being in Reception had made Sarah feel at home, walking into an emergency department would be like being surrounded by family. Losing her job *and* Karly had taken away an overwhelmingly large part of her life, hadn't it?

'Yes, *please*… I'd love that.' She bent to pick up the car seat and almost bumped heads with James, who was already holding the handle. They grinned at each other and then James led the way towards his department. She certainly did appreciate what looked like a very sleek setup, from resuscitation areas close to the ambulance bay entrance to one side to cubicles for less urgent patients on the other side of a well set up central area with multiple computer stations to access records and test results and a huge digital whiteboard that had all the information on every patient in the department, what the provisional diagnosis was, where they were and who was looking after them. A man with a white coat over his scrubs was standing in front of the board as a nurse in navy blue scrubs was pointing to something.

'That's Cameron Brown, our HoD,' James said. 'And that's our nurse manager, Jenny, he's talking to.' He greeted his colleagues as they got closer. 'This is Sarah,' he told them. 'I'm going to let her see whether the coffee here's any better than what she's used to in Leeds. She's a nurse practitioner in the ED there.'

'Ooh…' Jenny's smile was welcoming. 'I hope you're thinking of coming to work here. We're currently a wee bit short of nurses with your kind of qualifications.' But her attention shifted to the car seat before Sarah had the chance to respond. 'Who's this little angel?'

'This is Ivy.' Sarah could see the deep breath James was taking. Was he about to out himself as a father for the first time in public?

Yes…and there was a note of pride in his voice as he added to the introduction.

'Ivy's my daughter,' he said.

Cameron's eyebrows rose but his phone started ringing as he opened his mouth to say something and he took the call instead.

'Ah…have you come to check out the day care facilities?' Jenny was nodding as she smiled at Sarah, clearly assuming that she was Ivy's mother and James's partner.

Sarah couldn't help a sidelong glance. Would James put her straight? With a look that might give the impression that the idea was ludicrous?

'It's a fabulous creche,' Jenny said. 'I had both my kids in there since they were about this age until they started school and they absolutely thrived.' Her voice trailed into silence as she heard the tone in Cameron's voice and the rapid-fire questions he was asking.

'How far away? How many? Right…keep me posted. We'll be on standby.'

He ended his call. 'Major incident activation,' he said. 'A viewing platform in the Cairngorms somewhere near the path up to Ben Macdui has apparently collapsed and possibly more than twenty people have fallen about thirty metres into a gully. Police and Mountain Rescue are already on the way to the scene but we're the nearest trauma centre so we've been put on standby to receive any serious cases.' He eyed James. 'You've done disaster management training, haven't you?'

'I have. I'm qualified as a Medical Incident Officer and I've been involved with situations in both London and Europe. I've also had some HEMS training.'

'Perfect.' Cameron's nod was brisk. 'There's a helicopter being diverted from an Aberdeen Air Ambulance call and they'll be touching down on the roof in around ten minutes to pick up someone qualified to act as the MIO as part of the initial response and triage. Would you be prepared to go? We're the closest major trauma centre and I've got to put our plan into action, clear space in the department and get all relevant specialties on standby.'

'Of course.' But James was turning away from his HoD to nod in Sarah's direction. 'Sarah's got a MIMMS certification. I think she should come with me.'

Sarah's eyes widened. She could feel her heart rate pick up as adrenaline began to flood her body. The reason she'd come into the hospital in the first place was completely forgotten but the feeling of being where she belonged and wanting to be part of what was going on around her had just become a whole lot stronger. A pull that was almost impossible to ignore. All she'd need to do was provide her Personal Identification Number and they could quickly confirm her qualifications on the Nursing and Midwifery Council register.

But she shook her head without hesitating. 'I can't leave Ivy.'

'I'll take her up to the creche myself,' Jenny said. 'She'll be safe, I promise you. I'll take personal responsibility for that if the response goes on after creche hours.' The older nurse met Sarah's gaze and there was understanding there. And a plea. 'There are people out there in trouble and they need all the expert assistance we can provide. You've got more expertise than any other nurses I could send.'

'We need to get our kits and overalls and get up to the helipad, stat. Come with me...' It was James who was holding Sarah's gaze now. 'Please...?'

Sarah couldn't shake her head again. She could feel the beat of her heart in her throat as she stared back at James and thoughts flew past so rapidly they could only coalesce into a feeling rather than words. Whatever she'd thought of this man before she'd made the road trip from Leeds to find him in the first place was forgotten as convincingly as the reason she'd come to find him at his place of work today.

He had no reason to trust that she was good at

her job, other than what he'd learned about her as a person since she'd turned up on his doorstep, and yet she could see that he genuinely wanted to work with her.

That he trusted her…?

Wow…

That trust went both ways, didn't it?

This man might not have intended to become a father but the way he'd not only accepted Ivy into his life but was stepping up to meet both moral and practical responsibilities made him just the rock Sarah needed as she got to grips with the unknowns of her own new life. Someone she could trust to protect and care for Ivy as much as she intended to do.

Someone who had saved her own life and was asking her to help him do the same for others.

Okay… There was no way she could say no. Sarah grabbed her phone, handed the bag of baby supplies to Jenny, used a scrap of paper to scribble her full name and PIN for someone to check the nursing register and went after James, who had already turned away and seemed to know exactly where he was going.

'Wait…' she called. 'Wait for me…'

There was a wide walkway, with automatic doors at either end, that connected the emergency department to the ambulance bay. To one side of this corridor was a locked storage room beside a decontamination area but James had learned the code for this lock as part of his familiarisation with a new location.

'Here…' James lifted a small-sized pair of bright orange overalls from a hook and handed them to Sarah. 'Get these on.'

He pulled on a larger size himself, over his scrubs, zipped up the front and pulled on a fluorescent yellow vest with MEDICAL INCIDENT OFFICER emblazoned on a silver back panel.

'Here's a vest for you.' He handed Sarah one with NURSE on the back as she was slipping something into a pocket of her overalls. 'What are those?' he asked.

'Muesli bars. And glucose tablets. I always carry them.'

The glance Sarah slid in his direction looked wary. Did she think he might regret his decision to take her with him if she reminded him of her diabetes and the disaster of their first meeting? If anything, he was impressed by her attention to risk factors. They were heading into what would undoubtedly be a high-stress situation for an unknown length of time and possibly considerable physical exertion required. All these factors would affect Sarah's control of her blood glucose level but she was clearly in control, which meant it was one less thing he had to think about.

'I'll get the advanced care and drug kits. We'll both need one of those red rucksacks as well.'

'Are they standard issue first response kits?'

'Yes. I had a quick look when I checked this room out. They've got triage labels and pods colour-coded for "airway", "breathing" and "circulation". There are extensive dressing packs and there's saline and IV giving sets.'

All the basic requirements to keep someone's airway open, help them breathe if necessary and control major external haemorrhage. Other equipment and supplies would be available on ambulances and rescue aircraft. He worked rapidly along a shelf, handing Sarah a stethoscope that she slung around her neck, a radio that she clipped on and a logbook and water-resistant pen that went into a pocket. She grabbed a handful of disposable gloves from a box on the wall herself and shoved them into another pocket as they ran for the lifts.

The helicopter was landing as they reached the hospital roof. The sliding door on the side opened and a paramedic jumped out to make sure they could climb on board safely while the rotors were still running. It wasn't until he got close enough to hand them helmets that James recognised him.

'*Eddie…*'

He received a flash of a grin as well as a helmet. 'I thought it was about time we worked together, bro.' But Eddie was looking as surprised as James had been when he saw who was with him.

'*Sarah…?* You're working here now?'

'Just in the right place at the right time.' James could hear Eddie clearly over the noise of the rotors as he pulled on the helmet with its inbuilt audio equipment. 'She's got qualifications in major incident management as well as her nurse practitioner skills.'

The reminder of what had brought them all to this place at this time was enough to make anything personal irrelevant and James could see how focused Sarah was as she fastened the strap of her helmet and bent to pick up the rucksack beside her. She certainly looked the part with her hair tucked away under the helmet and wearing those overalls and vest, but it was more than simply a uniform. He could see that she understood exactly what they could be heading towards and there was a determination in her face that he was feeling himself.

It was a privilege to be allowed anywhere near a disaster scene, let alone become a part of an attempt to find and help any survivors. James knew, in that moment, that Sarah would push herself to do whatever it took to help those people and…

And he felt proud of her.

Jodie was part of the air ambulance crew and James and Sarah were introduced to the others as they sat down and buckled themselves in.

'This is Alex, who's our crewman, and Gus is our pilot.' Eddie gave a thumbs-up to Gus, who was watching to see the moment he was clear to lift off again. He pulled out a tablet as the helicopter took off. 'What's the latest sitrep, Alex?' he asked.

James turned away from watching the roof of the Queen Mother's Hospital fall away beneath them. He also wanted to hear what the most recent situation report was.

'The police have officially declared this a major incident.' Alex was holding another tablet. 'And we have an exact location.' He turned the tablet so that James and Sarah could see a map on the screen and he zoomed in by stretching it with his fingers. 'There's no road into the gully but there is a rough track that allows access by foot, which will probably take a good twenty minutes. We'll put you and Sarah down at the Casualty Clearing Station that's being set up on the nearest road and someone will take you in.'

'Unless I can find a place to put you down a bit closer to the scene,' Gus put in. 'We'll be winching Eddie and Jodie down, but if there's a flat spot close enough I can touch down and let you all out.'

'Fingers crossed.' Eddie nodded. 'That would save a lot of time. We want to get to anyone with critical injuries as soon as possible and we can expect anyone that's survived a fall like that to have some major trauma.'

James found himself meeting Sarah's gaze in the beat of silence that followed. How many survivors could be expected after such a catastrophic fall? How horrific would their injuries be?

She was scared.

Of course she was. James could feel a beat of the same kind of fear of the unknown himself.

But he also got a glimpse of the kind of courage this woman had. The ability to take on something, no matter how daunting it might seem, because…she could. Because it was the right thing to do.

Like raising a child who was, as far as she knew at the time, devoid of any biological family that might care about her.

That determination he already knew she had was being mixed with that courage now. He could even hear the way she pulled in a new breath and left any shadow of that fear behind.

'Has the type of incident been confirmed?' Sarah asked.

'Yes. It's a structure collapse and fall. It's a large group of outdoor education students— ages about eighteen to twenty-one. One of the tutors witnessed the incident and sounded the alarm. Apparently, they were all crowding onto the lookout because someone had a selfie stick and they wanted a photo of the whole group with the view in the background.'

There was another silent moment as they all imagined the horror as that platform gave way under too much weight.

'There are survivors,' Alex added. 'No estimate of numbers, though. Nobody's got to the scene yet but the tutor could hear shouts for help.'

'Hazards?' Sarah was obviously using the METHANE acronym to gather whatever information was available. They already knew it was officially a major incident and the exact location and type of disaster it was.

'Mostly the terrain. Like the rough ground, the river and potential fall of debris from above. We won't know whether there's any risk of secondary collapse of the platform until the fire service experts have had a look. Check with them re stability if they're on scene when you get there. Be very careful if they're not, okay?'

'We've already covered access,' Jodie added. 'Number of casualties is still unknown but there are twenty-three course attendees and a tutor that are currently unaccounted for.'

'Emergency services are getting every resource available mobilised. Police, fire, mountain rescue. Even the Red Cross. There are road ambulances on the way from as far away as Aberdeen but it'll take a while for them to arrive.'

'There are at least two other helicopters on the way,' Gus added. 'From Glasgow and Inverness. And a local pilot is going in to see what he can report. He's going to look for any possible landing spots along the river going in from Braemar.'

'Jodie will be the ambulance incident officer until someone more senior arrives,' Eddie said. 'But the longer she can actually treat patients rather than get caught up in admin, the better.'

James caught the gaze shared between his brother and the woman who was his partner both professionally and personally and he felt a squeeze in his chest that was tight enough to be painful.

The *respect* in that glance was palpable.

So was the love…

And, just for a split second, Eddie had a flash of realisation that took him back to the night of Mick's jilting and the vow the three brothers had made to stay uncommitted to one person in order to avoid heartache and get the most out of life. In this brief moment of time, however, as he caught the power of that glance James could not only understand why Eddie had broken that vow, he was deeply envious.

He wanted to know what it would feel like to be *that* close to someone.

Because he had the feeling that Eddie might have been the first to realise that they had got it wrong that night. That staying unattached to anyone other than each other could be what was *preventing* them getting the most out of life.

The thought evaporated as Gus spoke over other radio traffic.

'We'll be over Balmoral estate in a couple of minutes. When you see that you'll know we're nearly there.'

Sarah listened to the bleeps, occasional static and voices of incoming updates as they got closer to the mountains in the Cairngorms National Park. She saw small villages below, following the line of the winding river, and the unmistakable turrets and spires of Balmoral Castle, but the sounds and sights were no more than a background as the tension rose. She actually jumped when she heard a new note in Gus's voice.

'Here we go. That's the track we're after at three o'clock. It's running alongside and sometimes through that stream that feeds into the River Dee.'

The crew in the cabin all leaned to see down to the right side of the helicopter.

The roadside at the start of the track was a mass of blinking lights from all the emergency vehicles already on site. Police cars were blocking the road to any normal traffic and Sarah could see two fire trucks and an ambulance. A jeep with a flashing orange light and a roof rack laden with gear looked as though it would belong to a mountain rescue crew. She could see that the chain of command, headed by the police, was already working to accepted protocols. The inner cordon would be the start of that track to begin with, with the casualty clearing station in front of an ambulance loading station and then a space before the outer cordon where road cones were being placed to define lanes and control the vehicles moving in and out.

'The local guy reckons there's enough flat space where the track meets the edge of that stream to get you down on the outskirts of the scene,' Gus told them as they left the cordons behind and followed the walking track into the gully. 'And…there it is…' he said only moments later, slowing to a hover. 'Looks like you've got a welcoming committee.'

A group of uniformed people were moving back onto the track to get out of the way but it was still a tight space and they had to follow directions fast to get out of and away from the aircraft safely. James was out before Sarah and she was grateful that he turned and held out his hand to take hers. This was more than a bit scary.

'Keep your head down,' he reminded her. 'Here we go.'

The grip on her hand was tight enough to be reassuring and Sarah wasn't about to let it go as she bent double to run under the spinning rotors. Alex was going to unload their gear and they could pick it up when the helicopter had lifted again.

She went to let go of his hand when they caught up with Eddie and Jodie and the rescue personnel waiting on the track but it seemed as if he wanted to keep holding it for a heartbeat longer. Raising her gaze as she pulled in a deep breath, she found James looking down at her. She wanted to look away so that he wouldn't see that fear that was trying to bubble up again. What were they about to face?

Was she even capable of dealing with something this huge?

But it was already too late to shift her gaze. It felt as if James had already seen everything.

He didn't say anything aloud but he didn't need to. That look said it all.

You're not alone, Sarah... We can do this...

CHAPTER SEVEN

THE SCENE WAS like something out of a disaster movie.

High above them, at the top of a steep, rugged cliff, they could see the poles that had held the viewing platform, their jagged, broken ends like smashed teeth pointing into the void where people had been thrown. Some people had been thrown clear of the solid, flat wooden structure to fall onto boulders in and beside this fast-flowing section of the mountain stream. It was possible there could be people who had fallen—or jumped—onto the cliff further up but the suddenness and speed with which this catastrophe had unfolded meant that the majority of the group packed onto the wooden floor, against the rails that should have kept them safe, had stayed together and it might have only been in the last few seconds that the platform—the size of a small room—had tipped and then landed on top of both people and boulders.

The first responders to this scene, which probably included the people who had alerted emergency services and the first local volunteers and police who could get to this remote location quickly, had already tried to help and it looked as though they had stayed to try and comfort survivors. James could see someone kneeling beside a person lying on the ground near the stream and another who had an arm around someone who was sitting, their head bent enough to touch their chest.

His heart sank as James flicked his glance back to where the platform had landed. Parts of the structure had broken and were heavy enough to be pinning the still figures that could be seen at the edges. One section was clearly teetering on top of the largest boulders.

'It's not stable.' The fire officer, wearing a vest that designated him the officer in charge, broke the quiet moment as the medics took in their first impression of the scene and the hazards it might contain. 'Don't get close enough to touch it. We've got USAR trained firies who are on the track already, carting in the gear we need to keep you medics safe while you're working.' He glanced up. 'We've also got someone watching for any further debris falling, like those poles and the concrete blocks that will have anchored them. If you hear a long, unbroken blast on a whistle, move back fast, okay?'

James gave a single nod. He could feel the tension around him that was sharp enough to cut yourself on. He could hear the sounds of people in pain. He could almost smell the blood and fear. As a member of the medical team who could do something to help people who were suffering, he was desperate to get started. The so-called 'golden hour' for treating major trauma patients had already ticked well past so they couldn't afford to lose any more time, but that didn't mean they could rush towards the first victims they could see. There was a good reason why the protocol they needed to follow had what seemed like a slow start.

He took a pack of labels from his pocket and saw that Jodie also had one in her hands.

'Sieve and sort?'

James nodded again. 'You and Eddie start at the stream and move in. Sarah and I will start from the cliff.' James spoke over his shoulder to the fire officer as he began moving. 'Has anyone been seen further up?'

'Search and Rescue have sent a team up to abseil down when we give them the all-clear. We don't want any debris being dislodged until we're working here.'

The first tool of managing a scene like this was called the 'sieve'. It was a rapid walk-through the whole scene to assign priority for medical attention. The only reason they would do anything to a victim at this stage was to reposition them to make sure their airway was open before checking that they were breathing or apply a tourniquet to obvious external haemorrhage. James walked towards the cliff to where he'd seen the person sitting with one of the first responders providing comfort and reassurance to someone who looked to be only in her late teens.

'I could have walked out with her, but I thought it would be safer to keep her still until someone who knew what they were doing had checked her.'

James handed Sarah a green label with an elastic loop to attach to the girl's wrist. If a victim was walking or capable of walking, they received this label that gave them a delayed priority three.

'You're doing a great job,' James told the first responder. 'Keep her here for a bit longer. We're doing a rapid triage right now but a team will be assigned to come back and do a more thorough check on everybody very soon and they'll decide the best way to get everyone out.'

It was only a matter of a few steps to the crumpled figure of someone who was lying on their back, not moving and making no sound.

Sarah was slightly ahead of James and she crouched, tilting the man's head to ensure the airway was open. Then she put her hand on the man's diaphragm and her face close enough to be able to feel a breath on her skin.

'Breathing?' James asked.

'No.'

James handed her a black label. There was no time to get caught by the emotion of finding a young person who had tragically lost their life. They had to keep moving.

The next person they came to was also lying very still, unconscious, but she was breathing. James watched the slow rate at which her chest was rising and falling. It took only a few seconds to estimate how many breaths she would be taking in a minute.

'Respiratory rate of less than ten,' he said.

He handed Sarah a red label, which was the highest priority for receiving immediate medical attention, and she slipped the elastic band around the girl's wrist.

After assigning two more black cards they were getting closer to the platform and there was a person who was lying on their side with their eyes open. She gave what sounded like a stifled sob when she saw James and Sarah approaching.

James crouched beside her. 'What's your name, sweetheart?'

'Catherine…'

Her voice was quiet and her face was too pale,

but they couldn't yet take the time to do a thorough primary survey and find out what her injuries might be. James could already tell that her respiratory rate was within acceptable levels. He took her hand and pressed against a fingernail for a rough check of her circulation by watching for capillary refill. It took less than two seconds, which meant that while this patient still needed urgent medical attention, she could go into the second priority for the moment.

'Yellow card, Sarah,' he said. He knew that Catherine's condition could deteriorate at any time and make her a red card priority but he made sure his tone was reassuring. 'We're going to be back very soon to look after you, Catherine,' he said. 'I promise.'

By the time they met up with Eddie and Jodie at the central point of this disaster, where people lay trapped beneath the platform, more and more rescue personnel were arriving. Fire service members were carrying the heavy gear that was going to be needed to stabilise the platform and then cut it up to remove it, which would give medics access to a lot more victims—if any had survived. In his peripheral vision, James could see Eddie attaching a black label to the ankle of someone whose upper body was under the edge of the platform. He lay down to try and see beneath the obstruction.

'Can anyone hear me?' he called loudly.

There was only silence after his call. Could anyone have survived not only the fall but being crushed beneath something this solid? Eddie called again, however.

'If you can make any noise at all, calling or tapping will let us know where you are. We're not going anywhere until we get everybody out, okay?'

James could see several ambulance officers standing, with packs on their backs and other gear like oxygen tanks and defibrillators in their hands, where the track was at its closest to this section of the creek. Two more arrived who had their gear in a Stokes rescue basket and he could see how eager they were to be told who they could attend to first and who would need to be packaged for winching out by helicopter or carried out in the basket stretcher to where their ambulances would have been parked at the casualty clearing station.

It was the job of the medical incident officer to make those decisions. James could hear a helicopter approaching now and he knew that, if the resources were available, it would be preferable for anybody who'd been red or yellow carded to be stabilised and then winched from the scene. Chances of survival would be greatly increased by being flown to definitive care in an emergency department rather than delaying that journey by being carried for too long over a rough mountain track and then possibly have an ambulance transfer to get somewhere a helicopter could land. With the influx of rescuers and equipment now, it would be impossible to clear this area enough for someone to land where Gus had delivered his crew.

He turned back from his sweeping gaze of the scene to find Sarah watching him.

'You okay?' he asked quietly.

She nodded. James had already known that she would be fine but he'd needed to check. 'Stay here and work with Eddie,' he told her. 'Jodie and I need to step back and manage the resources we're getting, here. Jodie?'

Sarah watched James and Jodie walking to where the entrance point at the track was getting crowded with so many people and so much equipment. It was overwhelming to try and look down on this as a big picture and decide what needed to be done and who needed to be treated first and she was grateful she didn't need to be the one making those decisions.

How amazing was it that Ivy's father *was* the person who was capable of doing just that? Even the way James was holding himself as he walked—his shoulders back, walking as if he knew exactly where he was going and why—was enough to inspire confidence.

And deep, deep respect…

'Sarah…?' Eddie's voice was deceptively calm. He'd moved a piece of timber to get to someone further around the platform. 'Can you find a tourniquet in my kit, please? I've got a femoral bleed here and I don't want to take the pressure off.'

Unzipping the pack made a sound that Sarah would later remember marked what felt like the real start to this mission. When things got so busy that, looking back, it became a blur. There was a base layer of all the physical tasks she was completing, assisting paramedic teams as they assessed, treated and packaged patients for transport, but every one of her senses was overloaded with the enormity of the whole scene.

The volume and complexity of sounds was extraordinary. There were people near her asking for equipment or drugs to be found or something to be done, like keeping pressure on a bleeding wound or checking vital signs by taking a pulse or blood pressure. There were people shouting instructions further away, like the rescue crews who were trying to stabilise the platform by placing sloping metal struts that had a flat base and could telescope out with a rachet mechanism to fix themselves to whatever needed to be made secure. Occasionally there was the roar of a chainsaw or the deafening beat of helicopter rotors as an aircraft hovered to lower a stretcher and then winch a patient onboard and sometimes there was the heartrending cry of someone in terrible pain.

And those sounds, along with the dreadful injuries Sarah was seeing, added a layer of emotion to this experience that she knew she couldn't afford to even begin to process until this was over.

Jodie left the scene with one of the most critical red card patients they winched up to a helicopter. At one stage Sarah was helping Eddie as he assessed Catherine, who was still conscious but only just. She was confused about where she was and what had happened and her blood pressure was low enough to suggest she had some major internal bleeding going on. Eddie upgraded her priority to red and got her on the next helicopter that became available.

Sarah had seen James on more than one occasion but not to speak to. He was in one place and then another, checking on patients and directing new medical teams to where they were needed. He was talking to firemen and Search and Rescue people and at one point she saw him speaking to a team that then began the grim task of taking the fatalities away by stretcher, presumably to a temporary morgue until they could be identified and relatives informed.

James was much closer to Sarah when he came to watch a section of the platform being lifted clear, but she stayed where she was for a moment because she already knew that the first victim they would access was the person that Eddie had long ago attached a black label to. She watched James in the hope of catching his gaze. Perhaps he would tell her where she should go next, given that the number of medics on scene were now outnumbering the number of people needing their attention. Sarah had even found time and space to check her own blood glucose level, which was, amazingly, still within an acceptable range despite all the stress, but she made herself eat something anyway.

She was still watching James as the fire officers stepped back and she saw his face as he took in what he could see, which was, presumably, a tangle of bodies. The sombre moment seemed contagious enough for the general noise level to suddenly drop and it was in that quiet beat that Sarah heard what sounded like a cry.

A man revved the chainsaw, stepping in to tackle the next section of the platform, but Sarah waved at him.

'Stop,' she yelled. 'I think I heard something.'

James walked towards her. 'I was told this

whole area had been checked several times for any survivors.'

'I'm not sure,' Sarah admitted. 'But…it felt like someone was calling. From somewhere under the middle.'

James held up his arms. 'Can everyone be quiet, please? We need to be able to hear.'

The chainsaw was switched off. People stopped talking. Thankfully, there were no helicopters approaching or hovering right now.

Sarah knelt beside the smashed edge of the platform and peered beneath it to the narrow gap made by the boulders it was resting on. The torch on her helmet lit up the darkness and she gasped, lifting her head to find James right beside her.

'Oh, my God…there's someone here,' she told him. 'And she's alive…' She dropped flat again. 'Hey…' she called. 'I'm Sarah… What's your name?'

'Mika…'

Sarah had been doing so well keeping her own emotions under control, but this—finding someone alive when it seemed like all hope had been lost—brought tears to her eyes and a catch to her voice.

'We're going to get you out, Mika, okay?'

'Okay…'

Sarah shifted as she felt James squeeze closer

to be able to see what she could see, but there was a sound of distress from Mika.

'Don't go away…' she said. 'Sarah…?'

'I'm here, darling. I've got James with me. He's a doctor…'

'Mika?' There was a gentle tone in James's voice. 'Are you having any trouble breathing?'

'I…don't think so…'

'Does anything hurt?'

'My legs… There's something on top of them. Something really heavy…' Mika's voice broke in a sob. 'Please…help me… Get me out…'

There were people crowded behind where Sarah and James were lying on the ground.

'We could lift that section of the platform and give you access right now,' a fire officer said. He started to call instructions to his team, but James cut him off.

'No…wait…' James disappeared as he scrambled back to his feet.

Eddie was there as well and Sarah could just hear him explaining to the fireman why they had to wait to free this victim.

'She could have an extremely heavy weight on top of her legs. She's been under there for hours now.'

'If the weight gets lifted before we've treated her, she'll get the effects of something called crush syndrome,' James added.

He must have turned away or lowered his voice so that there was no chance of Mika hearing, but Sarah knew what he would be saying—that lifting a heavy weight from where it had been crushing a significant part of a human body could release toxins that could cause dysrhythmias and cardiac arrest. They needed to protect Mika from that danger by giving her intravenous fluids and drugs that would counteract the acid, myoglobin and potassium leaking out of dying muscle cells. Putting tourniquets on between the crushed area and the rest of the body could also help, but how were they going to be able to do any of that in this horribly limited space? Even someone Sarah's size would have difficulty getting close enough to touch Mika.

Or would they?

Sarah wriggled forward a few inches. And then a few more. Her helmet was scraping against wood but she had enough room to move her arms quite freely. She stretched out her hand. Mika stretched out hers and their fingers touched. A heartbeat later and Sarah was holding Mika's hand and there was no holding back emotion in this instant. Sarah hadn't felt like this since she'd held Ivy, moments after the baby had taken her first breath. Or when she'd held Karly, moments after *she* had taken her last.

'It's okay,' Sarah said, her voice raw. 'We're going to take care of you, Mika. We're going to get you out of here…'

James had seen the top of Sarah's body disappear beneath the edge of the platform and the sudden bolt of what felt like fear took him by surprise. She was putting herself in danger.

He didn't want anything to happen to her.

For Ivy's sake…

The fire officer was watching too. 'It's stable enough,' he said. 'If you can reach her to do what you need to do, that's all good. I'll get our guys in position to lift things off as soon as you give the go-ahead.'

James lay down again and tried to join Sarah in the space beneath the planks of wood but it took only seconds to realise he wouldn't be able to get anywhere near Mika. He could, however, talk to Sarah and reach far enough to pass her things. He had Eddie outside, who could deliver whatever he asked for. In this almost underground space it felt like they were cut off from the outside world, but there was strength to be found in not being alone here with someone who desperately needed their help.

He could do this. With Sarah.

They could do this.

'Can you get any vital signs?' he asked. 'A

heart and respiration rate? What's her radial pulse like?'

'She's breathing well,' Sarah told him. 'Heart rate's a hundred and ten but she's got a good radial pulse and steady rhythm. Mika? If no pain was zero and ten was the worst you could imagine, how would you score the pain in your legs?'

'Ten…'

'We'll give you something for that right now,' James promised. 'Sarah, can you get close enough to be able to administer some intranasal fentanyl as a starting point?'

'Yes… I think so.'

Eddie found a syringe and drew up the drug. James reached to put it in Sarah's hand.

'There's an atomiser on the end of the syringe. Get Mika to turn her head to one side if she can. Aim for the centre of the nasal cavity before pushing the plunger.'

Her fingers brushed his as she took the syringe. 'Okay.'

James could see how awkward it was for Sarah to move but she somehow made it look easy. 'What about getting IV access?' he asked. 'We need to get some fluids running. Intraosseous if we can't get a vein.'

'I've got good access to the elbow and hopefully Mika's blood pressure is enough for it not to be too hard to find a vein. Pass me a tourniquet?'

James handed her the tourniquet and then an alcohol wipe and a cannula. He held his own gaze steady to help give Sarah more light, so he saw the moment she got access to a vein and the skill with which she eased the cannula into place and then managed to secure it, all the while keeping up a steady stream of communication with Mika to let her know what she was doing.

'Keep your arm nice and still for me... Good girl...that's perfect. Sharp scratch now... There...all done. I'm just going to tape it on so it won't get pulled out. We'll be able to give you more medicine for that pain soon...'

She sounded so calm, James thought. As if she knew exactly what she was doing and had every confidence that it would work. If he was Mika, he would find it very reassuring. He would believe every word she said. He'd also seen the skill she'd already displayed in the work she was doing. He would believe she was capable of whatever she set her mind to achieving.

Eddie had a giving set primed and ready for James to give to Sarah to attach to the cannula plug.

'Find a pressure cuff to put on the bag of saline,' James reminded Eddie. 'We need to get several litres of fluid infused before we lift that weight so we'd better get on with it.'

There were drugs to be drawn up and administered as well. Sodium bicarbonate, calcium gluconate, nebulised salbutamol. There was pain control to keep on top of and James wanted Sarah to try and get ECG electrodes in place so they could monitor Mika's heart rhythm before, during and after the release of the weight.

It took time, but it was no surprise that Sarah was able to get the electrodes for a basic three-lead ECG in place on Mika's wrists and the sides of her abdomen and when the static subsided James was happy with what he could see on the screen. There were no warning signs of a dangerous level of acidosis or electrolyte imbalance like flat or missing P waves or peaked T waves.

'Sinus rhythm,' he told Sarah. 'Looking good.'

Something Sarah couldn't manage, however, was to get combat army tourniquets around the top of Mika's legs.

'There's a broken beam just over the iliac crest level. I can't reach past it far enough to be able to do anything.'

He could hear the effort in her voice. Pain, even.

'Don't keep trying,' he told her. 'We can be ready to put tourniquets on the moment we get clear access. We've got people positioned to take the weight and lift any time now. I'll give you a countdown…'

'Sarah?' There was an urgent tone in Mika's voice. 'I'm scared… What's going to happen?'

'They're almost ready to lift the bit that's trapping your legs. It'll be bright light that might hurt your eyes and it's noisy, with lots of people around. I think I can hear a helicopter that's not far away too, and that might be coming to take you to hospital, but don't be scared. I'm right here. I won't leave you.'

'Sarah can stay with you,' James promised. 'She can come with us when we take you to hospital.'

Mika was sobbing. 'Can she hold my hand?'

'Of course I can, hon,' Sarah said. 'Here it is… You hold mine too. As tight as you need to.'

James could almost feel that hold himself as Mika's distress lessened. A short time later, he took a deep breath. They were as ready as they could be.

'On the count of three,' he called a few minutes later. 'One…two…*three*…'

The tension ramped up the instant the weight came off Mika's legs and rescuers were able to get to her. Sarah stayed lying beside her patient, amongst the rocks and broken timber, so she didn't have to let Mika's hand go as other medics moved in to take over her care and get her ready to be winched clear of the scene of this terrible incident. The monitors that would set off alarms if there were any signs that her condition was suddenly deteriorating after the removal of the weight were reassuringly quiet.

James let out the breath he hadn't realised he was holding and looked away from the screen back to Sarah. Did she realise that all the work she had done to help prepare Mika for this next phase of her rescue had paid off? That she might have played the biggest part in saving a life, here?

Sarah had streaks of dirt and blood and possibly tears on her face and she was squinting in the glare of daylight but, as she looked up to catch his gaze, there was a hint of a smile there as well.

A nanosecond of private communication just between them before the controlled chaos of continuing and extending Mika's treatment began.

We did it...

And in that same moment that was no more than a passing flash, James remembered again that he'd once thought he would never have noticed Sarah Harrison if their paths had crossed on a busy street. That she wasn't remotely like the gorgeous women he'd always chosen to get closer to.

This time, however, despite the way she was looking right now, James knew exactly how wrong he had been. Sarah wasn't simply special, or skilled, or impressive in the things she could do or her attitude to life.

She was absolutely stunning.

With that amazing ability the brain had to register emotions that covered so much detail in such a tiny fragment of time, James was also aware of something else.

Relief?

That Sarah Harrison would never appreciate, let alone reciprocate, any kind of attraction. Ivy was the person who mattered above all else in any relationship he was going to have with Sarah and life was complicated enough already, wasn't it? He was a father now, for heaven's sake, and he had to learn to juggle new responsibilities with the work that he had devoted his adult life to so far. He had a brother coming home very soon who would need considerable support for the foreseeable future. His social—and sex—life felt no more important than a distant memory.

Priorities had changed so much that major parts of his life were unrecognisable. Thank goodness some things hadn't changed. Like the focus needed to get a critically ill patient into an emergency department and, most likely, into Theatre in order to save her life.

Sarah was still holding Mika's hand as the paramedic crew worked to splint and dress her badly crushed legs so that she could be transferred to a stretcher. One that was being lowered from the Aberdeen Air Ambulance helicopter that was hovering directly overhead, so that had to be Jodie who was bringing it down. Eddie would want to travel back with the last patient he was treating who needed to be evacuated and there was no reason for James to stay on scene any longer either.

He could end an experience he was going to remember every detail of for the rest of his life in the same way he'd started it.

With Sarah…

CHAPTER EIGHT

THE BEEPING OF her phone to announce the arrival of a new text message was becoming a welcome sound.

The first message had arrived almost as soon as Sarah had carried Ivy inside after getting her home from the hospital as darkness fell.

Is Ivy okay?

Sarah had texted back.

All good. People in the creche awesome. They stayed late when they knew we were on our way back. How's Mika doing?

In CT. Theatre on standby.

Keep me posted.

A 'thumbs-up' emoji appeared on her screen. Sarah got the fire going, carried a now grizzly Ivy into the kitchen and managed to make herself a slice of toast and prepare a bottle for the baby virtually one-handed.

'We both need to eat,' she explained. 'And sleep. I don't think I've ever been this tired in my life.'

But she wouldn't have missed any of it, Sarah thought as she settled herself on the couch, smiling at Ivy's contented snuffling as she attached herself to the bottle and got stuck into her dinner.

'Your daddy wasn't wrong,' she murmured. 'You are a wee piglet.' She took a large bite of the peanut butter toast and then reached for her phone as it beeped again.

CT scan suggests one leg can't be salvaged. Maybe both.

Oh, no. Poor Mika.

She's still alive. Cardiac and renal function okay.

I feel bad I didn't stay. I promised I would.

She was intubated by the time you left. She didn't notice, I promise.

James had added a smiley face emoji.

I'm going to come home soon myself. Surgery might take hours.

Good thinking. You must be exhausted.

There was a short silence then, and Sarah put the phone down to shift Ivy's weight and tilt the bottle to a better angle. The new beeping was a surprise because she thought the conversation had finished.

You were amazing today, Sarah. I'll bet Mika will never forget the person who was brave enough to be under there with her and do what it took to save her life.

Sarah found herself blinking back tears as she responded.

You were there too, you know.

Not likely to ever forget...

This time the silence was longer and Sarah used it to scroll a news feed which linked her to a broadcast about the tragedy in the Scottish mountains today.

'There are six people in hospital,' a newsreader announced. 'The number of fatalities has risen to twelve, but that may go up. Three of the young victims are in serious or critical condition in the Queen Mother's Hospital in Aberdeen.'

Sarah hadn't noticed anyone with cameras at the scene today but she was seeing footage of the crowd of rescue workers and a helicopter in the distance overhead. And then she saw a large section of that platform being lifted and there *she* was…lying on her stomach, holding Mika's hand.

Good grief…she was barely recognisable as she turned to blink at the brighter light but Sarah could remember that moment so vividly. She could remember seeing James and the wash of emotion that had to be the peak of what had been an overwhelming experience that they had been through together. She'd known that they had forged a bond in the last few hours that would link them for the rest of their lives—even if they weren't already linked, thanks to Ivy.

This was a much more personal bond that was just between the two of them. One that had underscored that trust she already had in James, but this was more than knowing he would protect and care for Ivy.

It almost felt as if she was under that umbrella of protection. Not just because he'd pulled her through that hypoglycaemic crisis the first night they'd met—any doctor would have done that.

No… Feeling like this was part of a new bond too. Because Sarah would never forget the way he'd looked at her after they'd walked around as they began the triage on that horrific scene together and the first thing he'd asked was whether *she* was okay.

Oh, help... Emotions were threatening to do her head in right now. Sarah swiped her screen to end the images that were taking her back to the scene. Ivy's lips were slack around the teat of the bottle so she put it down beside her half-eaten toast and moved Ivy upright onto her shoulder to rub her back.

The baby's burp made her remember the first time James had done this. His laughter and that grin on his face.

The tears that were escaping now felt like happy ones, but it was a warning that Sarah needed to keep an eye on herself. She should probably check her blood glucose levels and have more to eat.

Oddly, it was right at that moment that her phone beeped again.

Have you eaten? I could pick up some Thai food or a pizza on the way home.

Sarah sent back the emoji of lip-licking.

Pizza please. Calzone is my favourite.

It felt as if he was going home.

To be with the most important people in his life, even.

How weird was that?

He'd had no idea that Sarah Harrison even existed such a short time ago and he certainly hadn't dreamed that he had a child of his own.

It all felt a bit too emotional as James pulled into the driveway of what was, he reminded himself, his sister's home, not *his*.

His head was all over the place, to be honest. He'd seen too much, done too much and felt way too much over too many hours and he was totally exhausted, physically, mentally and emotionally.

He was also starving and the smell of the wood-fired pizzas on the passenger seat of his sister's car was driving him nuts, although they were nowhere near as hot as they had been when he'd collected the takeaway order. It would be very easy to heat them up again in the oven, however, and James was feeling good about being able to do something for Sarah, who had to be just as wrung-out as he was. Providing a meal was a basic but always welcome gesture of caring for someone.

It was even better to offer a favourite meal.

'These guys apparently make the most authentic pizzas in Aberdeen,' he told her as he carried the boxes inside. 'And I have some red wine. Because you can't eat Italian without some red wine, right?'

Sarah was smiling. 'I do believe I've heard that rule somewhere.'

'Did you get my text about putting the oven on?'

'I did. It's hot.'

'Let's get these pizzas warming up, then. And find some wine glasses.'

It was Sarah who found the cupboard where the wine glasses were stored. She was standing on tiptoe to reach them as James closed the oven door, after putting the pizzas on a baking tray. He straightened up to find he was suddenly standing far closer to Sarah than he had expected. Bumping her arm, in fact.

'Oops…sorry.' James could see what she was doing now. 'Let me get those glasses for you.' He reached up but Sarah still had her arm there and he bumped her again. And then they did a version of those awkward, impromptu dance moves that happened when you were in the street trying to avoid a stranger's path but you both moved in the same direction.

Sarah laughed and stopped moving.

So did James.

And then, for what felt like a very long moment, they simply looked at each other. Sarah looked as tired as he felt. And…

'Did you realise you still have mud on your face?'

'What? I washed it.'

'Well, it is kind of hiding, I guess.' James touched the streak on the angle of Sarah's jaw, just below her ear, that ran into her hair.

He knew instantly that he shouldn't have done that. But how could someone's skin generate a sensation that felt like actual electricity? James had never felt anything quite like that in his life. It seemed like Sarah might have also been aware of the sensation. She had already stopped moving but now it felt as if she had just frozen. As if she was totally shocked by his touch.

James dropped his hand, but not quite fast enough. Or perhaps it was the fact that he'd made eye contact with Sarah that was making this suddenly so intense? Under this light it looked as if that rich hazel colour had flecks of gold in it. Like stars, or fragments of sunshine. Her lips were slightly parted and...

And all James could think of for one heartbeat, and then another, was touching those lips with his own so that he could find out if they were as soft and delicious as they looked.

Good grief... He needed to get a grip. He also needed to break that eye contact before Sarah could have any idea what was running through his overtired brain.

'Sorry,' he murmured again. Then he took a breath. 'Right. Glasses. Wine. Let's go and sit by the fire for a few minutes until our dinner's warm enough.'

'Yes, let's.' Sarah was turning away.

She touched her face herself as she did so, her fingers finding the patch that marred the softness of her skin. Astonishingly, James could feel a faint aftershock of that jolting sensation, as if he was touching her skin again himself.

'I had no idea I'd missed that bit of dirt.' Sarah shook her head. 'I was waiting to have a proper shower and wash my hair after Ivy was settled.'

She was speaking quickly, as if she needed a distraction. Or perhaps she was determined to ignore the possibility that an irresponsible playboy and/or a sex addict might have just made some kind of move on her?

And that was just what James needed to flick off the unacceptable switch of feeling physically attracted to Sarah. He didn't want to prove her right.

'You never got a chance to show me those pictures of the house you looked at this morning. Can you send me the link to the website?'

'I've probably still got it open on my browser.' Sarah picked up her phone. 'Yes…it's right here. Look…'

They sipped the excellent red wine he'd opened as James scrolled through images on a website and then they ate the delicious calzone pizzas with their crisp, egg-washed and parmesan-dusted dough encasing pepperoni and fresh mozzarella, onion, spinach and mushrooms.

'This is *so* good.' Sarah sighed.

'This house is so good.' James was having another look at the images. 'It's not far at all from where Eddie and Jodie are living.'

'Really? I'd like that,' Sarah said. 'It would be good to be in the city as well. I mean, I love being out in the country but when you're on your own with a baby it can get a bit…lonely…sometimes.'

Of course it could. Especially when you were grieving the loss of a friend who was as close as a sister. Maybe grieving the loss of a chosen lifestyle as well. Having worked so closely with Sarah today, James knew how good she was at her job and that she had the same kind of passion for her work as he did himself.

'The house is close to Queen's. That's a bonus too.'

After today, it was obvious that Sarah could easily fit in with his new department. Was it possible that Sarah might consider a move to Aberdeen, even? No…he was getting ahead of himself. James didn't even have a permanent job at Queen's himself. They needed to take this journey one step at a time.

'Three bedrooms,' he added. 'And two of them have ensuite bathrooms…' He found a smile as he glanced sideways in time to catch Sarah eating the last bite of her pizza. 'That's one each for you and me and Ivy could have the one without the bathroom.'

'It's quite expensive…' Sarah chased down her bite of food with some wine. 'But I do have someone I used to work with in Leeds who's keen to take over Karly's room in the apartment we shared. She's going to pack up some more clothes and things and send them up to me by courier so I don't have to do that drive again just yet.'

'That's helpful. It's a long drive.'

'It wouldn't work long-term because I'll need that room for Ivy, but it will give her the time to find somewhere else. And she'll pay for the room, which means I could help with the rent of this place for as long as I'm here.'

James shook his head. 'You're not going to pay any rent,' he said firmly. 'The house I move into is going to be my home for the foreseeable future.' He waited for Sarah to lift her gaze and meet his and he spoke carefully. 'I want you— and Ivy—to feel as if it's your home as well. For now,' he added, to dilute any pressure his words might imply. 'And for whenever you visit later maybe, until we decide what we're going to do long-term.'

He broke the eye contact to check his watch. 'I don't think it's too late to call the agent.' He tapped the phone's screen. 'If it's still available, let's find out just how fast we could make this happen. We need to find somewhere before Ella and Logan get back home.'

He ended the call a short time later as Sarah came back from carrying their dirty dishes into the kitchen. 'The house is currently empty and the lease could be taken over as soon as the paperwork is signed and the fees paid. I've asked for an option to be held for me until tomorrow afternoon. The agent's going to be there at midday to get the meter read and I said I'd come and have a quick look on my way to work and make a decision then. It's good timing. There's a departmental meeting first thing, which is a debrief for today's major incident response so I need to be there, but I'm not starting my shift until two o'clock.'

'I'll be in town then too. I've got an appointment for Ivy's vaccinations at a medical centre at eleven o'clock. Could I come and have a look with you? I'd love to see inside the house.'

'Of course… I wouldn't want to take the house if you found you hated it.'

'I won't hate it.' Sarah sounded quite sure. 'I think I love it already.'

James could feel some of the emotional over-load of the day lifting at the prospect of some-thing positive on the horizon. 'Sarah…?'

Her glance was curious. 'Yeah…?'

'Thank you…'

Did she realise that he was thanking her for more than finding a house they could share for the next little while? That her willingness to give him time to adjust to being a father and rede-fine his life was… Well, it was a gift, that was what it was.

Sarah's smile was shy, as if she was embar-rassed by his appreciation.

'I'm going to go and have a shower,' she told him, scrambling to her feet. 'Apparently I have dirt on my face…'

The hot water was rinsing away any visible rem-nants of the day, along with the shampoo bubbles that were streaming down Sarah's body, mak-ing her skin feel slippery as she brushed them away. She closed her eyes and let it rain directly on her face to simply enjoy the sensation of the warmth and water for a moment longer.

Except it wasn't really the water she was thinking about, was it?

It was the memory of James touching that soft

skin on her neck, just below her ear. That spear of sensation that had shot straight into the core of her body that probably had a lot to do with the look he was giving her. As if he wanted to *kiss* her…?

A look he'd probably given women a thousand times over the years so it was no wonder he was so good at it.

It was no wonder Karly had succumbed to it either. She wouldn't have had the slightest hesitation in grabbing that moment in the kitchen and letting James kiss her. She could almost hear her friend's voice as a whisper in her ear.

'You need to live a little, Sass. We both know how short life can be…'

Sarah shifted just enough for the needles of hot water to be hitting her breasts instead of straight onto her face. What would it be like, she wondered, to be more like Karly and embrace moments in life like that?

To let someone, who was in no way a candidate for a meaningful relationship of any kind, kiss her senseless? Make love to her, even…?

Would she discover what other people seemed to find so compelling about sex that had, so far, totally passed her by?

Oh, my… Sarah shut the water supply off in the hope of shutting off that particular line of thought. She'd never broken the rules she'd made for herself regarding men. They were as iron-clad as the rules she had developed for managing her blood glucose levels and healthy eating regime.

Pizza and wine had been a bit of a treat but that was okay.

Sex with James Grisham would not be okay. He was Ivy's father and this whole situation was quite complicated enough. Sarah wrapped a towel around her body as she realised she hadn't brought the soft leggings and oversized tee shirt she wore as sleepwear into the bathroom. She picked up another towel to squeeze some of the dampness out of her hair as she left the bathroom.

And then she realised she'd left her phone downstairs because James had been using it to call the estate agent about the house. Without thinking, she opened her door, planning to dash downstairs and retrieve her phone so she could make sure she hadn't missed an alert about her glucose levels.

The last thing she expected to see was James standing right in front of her, with only a towel wrapped around his waist, his skin still glistening with moisture. He'd washed *his* hair too, and it was sleek against his head in dark tousled curls. He hadn't shaved so his jaw was shadowed and…and so damn *sexy*…

Sarah dropped her gaze so that she could make contact with his eyes because she knew he would be able to tell exactly what she was thinking, but now she could see the definition of muscles in those bare arms and the gorgeous olive colour of his skin. And...

And she could see her phone in his hand.

'I thought you might need this,' James said. 'My bad. I just remembered I'd been using your phone to call the agent, not mine.'

Oh, man...

Had this been the biggest mistake James had ever made?

He could see way too much of Sarah's skin. He could feel the soft heat of it. Worse, he could *smell* it and it was the most compelling aroma ever...

He heard a tiny sound which might have been Sarah trying—and failing—to say something. Or was it Ivy, stirring in her bassinet in the far corner of this large bedroom?

The thought that this might be a very good time for Ivy to wake up and demand attention slid through the back of his mind so fast it simply evaporated. Because it was at that moment that Sarah looked up at him and the heat between them was enough to be melting something.

Common sense, perhaps?

That thought didn't gain any traction either. Because James knew that Sarah was feeling this heat just as much as he was. The way her pupils had dilated so much it made her eyes look black suggested that she was perfectly well aware of what was hanging so palpably in the air between them. He remembered that moment in the kitchen when he'd first thought of kissing her and the desire to do so had been like nothing he was familiar with. Had that astonishing intensity been there because of what Sarah was thinking—and feeling? That she had wanted to kiss *him*? Despite her opinion of his past history with women? Or was it because of it?

Because she knew that this didn't have to be a big deal. That they were two people who were seriously attracted to each other. Two people who'd shared an extraordinary—and exhausting—experience today and were both too tired to worry about a bigger picture. Maybe they needed the escape. Or the joy of something so life-affirming?

But still, James hesitated.

Until he saw a big droplet of water from her wet hair escape and trickle down her forehead to catch on her eyebrow. It was a purely instinctive action to lift his hand and use his thumb to brush the drip away before it could get any closer to her eyes. His gaze never left hers and, beneath that tiny skin-to-skin contact, James could actually feel Sarah leaning into his touch as she let her eyelids begin to drift shut.

He slid his hand into the warmth of her damp hair to cradle the back of her head and watched her lips part as she tilted her head in invitation for the kiss that was as inevitable as taking his next breath.

But still, James held back. He bent his head enough to touch his forehead to Sarah's. He turned it so that his cheek could feel the side of her head without actually touching it. He let his nose brush hers as softly as a feather and he would have done it all over again except for the whisper of a sigh from Sarah that sounded like surrender.

Or maybe it was the sound of some kind of key being turned. A lock being opened.

An invitation for both of them to step into a totally private place?

He brushed his lips against hers. Once... twice...

The third time he let them settle, his whole body tuned to the tiniest nuances in Sarah's response that would tell him, far better than any words, whether this was something she really wanted as much as he did.

It was a long, long moment before James broke that contact in order to take a breath.

And this time he was the one to let it out in a sigh that was, most definitely, complete surrender...

CHAPTER NINE

IT MUST BE TRUE.

Practice really did make perfect, didn't it?

How else could James be so good at making something so world-rocking as far as Sarah was concerned seem like nothing particularly out of the ordinary?

It probably helped a lot, mind you, when the sound of his phone ringing floated up the stairs in that space of time where they were both beginning to catch their breath after the most intense sexual experience Sarah had ever had in her life.

'I'd better get that.' He dropped a quick kiss on Sarah's forehead. 'I asked them to let me know when Mika got out of Theatre.'

James had his towel wrapped around his waist again when he returned to sit on the side of Sarah's bed a short time later.

'She's in Recovery,' he told her.

'How is she?'

'Stable. They're ready to transfer her to the

intensive care unit.' But there was a catch in his voice. 'She's lost one leg. Transfemoral amputation. She's going to need more surgery on the other leg, including a full knee replacement, but the surgeons are cautiously hopeful they can save it.'

Sarah could feel them both being sucked back onto the rollercoaster of this extraordinary day and the crash from the high point she was falling from, after James had just physically taken her somewhere she had never quite believed really existed, felt like it could be devastating. But James caught—and held—her gaze.

'You okay?'

Two tiny words. The same words he'd used at the scene today, after those awful first minutes when they had begun their daunting task of dealing with death and disaster. When he'd made her feel as though he cared about how she was feeling. There was time, now, to feel the squeeze on her heart with the thought that there was still someone in the world who really cared about her. It was enough to change the angle of that rollercoaster and put the brakes on that fall.

'She's alive,' Sarah said quietly. 'And that's a bit of a miracle so…yeah… I'm okay.'

But James was still holding her gaze and Sarah could sense the undertone to his query. Was he checking in to make sure she wasn't upset about the dramatic change that had just occurred in how well they knew each other?

She wasn't. Sarah had willingly taken the risk of breaking her own rules and wondering if she could be more like Karly and it was fair to say it had been a very successful experiment. All she needed now was to channel a bit more of Karly to be able to handle the aftermath so it didn't create any issues that might affect them being able to share the parenting of Ivy in any way.

This wasn't a situation Sarah had ever been in before but instinct told her to keep it light. To give James—or perhaps both of them—the chance to escape by making it clear that it had been a one-off?

So she made a face as she blew out a sigh. 'It's been quite a day, hasn't it?'

'Sure has.'

'Are *you* okay?'

'Never better.' There was something in his eyes that was definitely a compliment but Sarah pretended not to notice.

'You must be as tired as I am.' Her lips curled into just more than a hint of a smile. 'We were exhausted already but then we threw some wine and sex into the mix.' Her smile widened a little. 'What were we thinking?' The smile was fading now. 'But…thank you,' she whispered.

He didn't ask what she was thanking him for.

Maybe he thought it was for simply asking if she was okay after the news about Mika. Or for his support during the gruelling hours of being part of that disaster scene today.

Or might he have guessed it was for making love to her as if she was the most beautiful, *desirable*, woman in the entire world? As if the feel and taste of her body was all he could ever want. As if everything she'd been brave enough to do back to him had been better than anything he'd expected?

It didn't matter. She had let him know she appreciated any or all of those things. And she'd offered him a way out. She'd let him know that she could be like Karly and not make their sexual encounter any more significant than it was intended to be. That it had been a combination of factors that had led to something that neither of them had planned and she had no expectations that it was going to happen again.

James seemed to have got the message because he smiled back at her. 'I should be thanking you…' Then he leaned in and cupped her head with his hand, tilting it so he could press a kiss onto Sarah's hair. 'Sleep well…'

'What's her name?'

'Ivy.' James was carrying the car seat after helping Sarah get it out of her car.

'She's so *cute*.' The estate agent, Maureen, unlocked the front door of the stone house in Ferryhill. 'I absolutely adore that hair. How old is she?'

'Eight weeks.' It was Sarah who answered this time. She cast an anxious glance at Ivy and reached to make a tiny adjustment to the fuzzy pink blanket tucked around her. Taking her for all those vaccinations had been more stressful than she had anticipated, but Ivy seemed to be coping remarkably well now that the poking with needles and having to swallow nasty-tasting liquid was over with.

'This is the perfect family home,' Maureen said happily. 'I can't wait for you to see the garden.'

The hallway was wide enough for a bicycle to be propped against a wall.

'No problem to fit a pram in here,' Maureen pointed out. 'And so many lovely walks to go on with the river tracks not far away and Duthie Park just down the road. Imagine how good it will be, having picnics there in the summer—or maybe a birthday party for wee Ivy in the playground in years to come? They've got magic fairy houses there.'

James shared a glance with Sarah that took a moment to interpret. Was he apologetic or slightly horrified that Maureen was assuming they were a couple with the baby they shared?

Had she been mistaken in thinking that James, thanks to all that practice of being the perfect playboy, had been able to make it remarkably easy to smooth over any awkwardness of some rather large personal boundaries having been crossed? That perhaps the thought of being seen as a couple was enough of a shock for such a committed bachelor to make James regret what had happened last night?

She hadn't had that impression first thing this morning. James had certainly been in a bit of a hurry this morning to get into work for that departmental meeting, but he'd come into the kitchen to grab a coffee while Sarah was feeding Ivy and it had felt—almost—as if nothing had changed.

Ivy had even unleashed one of her loud burps having finished her breakfast and it had become an automatic trigger to make eye contact with James and share a smile. And yes…there might have been a deeper level to that eye contact and smile, but Ivy was grinning at them both and Sarah had definitely felt a wash of something like pure relief.

She was okay.

They were okay…

She didn't want James to start regretting what had happened between them.

Sarah certainly wasn't going to regret it.

Hopefully, her casual shrug would reassure him that she wasn't bothered by Maureen's assumption. It would have been odd if she hadn't thought they were Ivy's parents and were interested in renting this house as a family home. And Sarah wasn't about to tell a complete stranger what the unusual relationship was between herself and James.

She wasn't exactly sure she knew precisely what it was herself now.

She tried to seem engrossed, taking in all the features of the lovely sitting room they entered, with the polished wooden floor, high ceilings and the old register grate with the brightly coloured, flower-patterned tiles set into the cast-iron frame. What she was really thinking about, however, was the most amazing night of her entire life.

Who knew that sex could be *that* good?

That there didn't need to be any awkwardness or embarrassment or disappointment that lingered long after that particular milestone in a relationship was reached?

Okay… Sarah gave her head a tiny shake as she followed Maureen and James out of the sitting room and through a dining area that led into a large kitchen, making the ground floor of this house a very attractive, light-filled open-plan living space. She looked down at the beautiful flagstone floor but she was actually giving herself a firm reminder that, even in her imagination, she needed to correct her terminology.

She wasn't in any kind of romantic relationship with James. Even if that phone call hadn't interrupted the afterglow last night, she couldn't imagine that there would have been any romantic cuddling going on. It had only been about the sex.

And even if they ended up having sex every night for as long as she was in Aberdeen—the thought of which sent a rather delicious thrill down the length of Sarah's spine—any new dimension to the partnership they'd been thrown into was...

Temporary, that was what it was.

Sarah was still tired today, but she made an attempt to focus on this house tour in case James wanted to discuss it later. Upstairs, there were two charming bedrooms with sloping walls and dormer windows, one of which looked out over a private back garden. There was a wooden bench to sit on, against a background of hydrangea bushes with bright blue flowers, and a tree in front of it with a branch that curved over the grass and...

'There's a swing,' she said in delight.

'Isn't it perfect?' Maureen beamed. 'I knew you'd love it.'

It *was* perfect. Sarah could see herself sitting on that bench with James sitting beside her. They were both watching Ivy—who was big enough to be bending her little legs and pushing them out to make herself swing. Sarah could almost catch a glimpse of a dog lying close to the trunk of the tree.

The bubble of the idyllic family scenario popped a heartbeat later as Maureen ushered them towards the master bedroom suite. It wasn't going to happen, was it? At some point, Sarah was going to return to her own life and the job she had in Leeds. And yes, maybe James had suggested that he might be up for moving to Leeds, but that would depend entirely on where he was able to find a permanent job. And with all his family here in Aberdeen it seemed very unlikely that he'd want to move right out of Scotland.

James seemed to be standing very still as he stood and looked at a very pretty bedroom that boasted a chandelier and built-in wardrobes. Was he thinking of how much room there was for sharing that bed? Was he wondering whether life would return to normal once Sarah and Ivy had returned to Leeds and would only be visiting? It was quite possible James was looking forward to having that kind of distance between them.

It didn't matter how good the sex had been, did it? Or that Sarah would be quite prepared to trust James with her life. He was not the kind of man who would ever be content to be confined in a traditional monogamous relationship and nuclear family and he was most certainly not the kind of man that Sarah had been looking to share *her* life with. Like those reliable, predictable men she had dated in the past and, for a chosen few, had gone to bed with.

Not one of them had ever taken her to paradise and back again, like James had done with such apparent ease last night.

As if he caught the gist of her thoughts, James threw a glance over his shoulder and Sarah suddenly knew that he'd actually been thinking about her as he'd been looking at that bed. What was even more disconcerting was that the look in his eyes also told her that he was more than up for doing it all over again. If she was...

Oh, help... Sarah could feel herself blushing. Just as well Maureen was looking down at Ivy again.

'Look at those red wee cheeks,' she said. 'Is it too warm for you in here, my love?'

It was too warm for Sarah, that was for sure.

She stepped out of the main bedroom and a few steps took her to the top of the staircase. Something made her turn her head sharply—as if she'd seen something at the bottom of the stairs.

Or some*one*? It was clearly her imagination that was playing tricks on her.

Making her think that Karly had been standing at the foot of these stairs. Giving her a thumbs-up signal, even? Showing her approval of how Sarah had broken the rules and taken a leaf out of her own book, anyway.

Giving her permission to enjoy it as long as it lasted, perhaps?

'Live a little more, Sass... You know you want to.'

Ivy started to cry before they left the house.

'Call or text me,' Maureen said outside, handing her card to James. 'As soon as you've had a chance to talk with each other and make a decision. I've got another appointment to get to.'

She probably wanted to get away from the now shrieking baby. The sound was just what Sarah needed to jolt her out of dreaming of a future that included this family house with its swing in the garden and to stop her thinking about last night and any repercussions, including the temptation to repeat the experience. Nothing other than the present was of any importance right now. She had an unhappy baby to look after.

One who did, indeed, have very red cheeks even though they were outside in much cooler air.

'She feels a bit hot.' Sarah took the blanket off Ivy as James put the cocoon into the middle of her back seat.

'It's probably just a reaction to the vaccinations. Have you given her some paracetamol?'

'No... I was planning to give her some as soon as we got home.'

'Come past Queen's. We've got buckets of liquid paracetamol. I'm sure you'd rather have her settled before you drive home? It'll be a lot more effective if we give it to her before she gets any more miserable.'

'That's true. I could give her a feed too. That might help settle her.'

'We could feed ourselves too, if you like? I've got plenty of time before I need to start work and I've discovered the cafeteria does the best mac and cheese ever, with extra crispy breadcrumbs on the top.'

He licked his lips and Sarah felt a spear of sensation that went straight into the core of her body with enough force to be actually painful.

'Might have to see what Ivy thinks about that idea.'

James nodded. 'I'll meet you in the car park. I'll give Maureen a call on the way. I'm thinking I should take a short-term lease, at least. What do you think? It's perfect, isn't it?'

'I do love it,' Sarah admitted.

'So do I.'

Oh...

Something in his eyes was suggesting that James was thinking about that master bedroom again. The kick deep in her belly wasn't painful this time but Sarah hastily turned back to fastening the seatbelt attachments to Ivy's car seat before James could see any reflection of that desire in her own eyes.

'It's going to be your house,' she reminded him, keeping her tone deliberately light. 'It really only matters what *you* think.'

If his period of living in Aberdeen had followed the plans James had originally made, he would have been about to take over Eddie's basement apartment with Ella and Logan due to arrive home within days. He hadn't dreamed he would be agreeing over the phone to sign up for at least a six-month lease on what was a very grown-up sort of house in a very nice suburb in the city.

A family sort of house.

With three bedrooms, one of which had a very big bed.

A house that he was intending to share with Sarah Harrison for as long as she was prepared to stay on in Aberdeen herself. How much of her six-month maternity leave had she already used up? Two months, probably, if she'd started when Ivy was born but before Karly had died. That left four months.

Four months was a long time.

James pushed his hair back with his fingers as he paused at a red traffic light. Four months was way longer than James had ever dated anybody—even the ones that he could totally trust not to expect anything more than a 'friends with benefits' arrangement. If he was honest, he preferred the sort of night he'd had with Karly. Great fun but only ever going to be for a night or two.

He would never have picked Sarah as someone who was okay with casual sex.

But then he would never have guessed that she could be such an intoxicating mix of innocence and red-hot passion. Vulnerability mixed with a determination to hold nothing back in either giving or receiving pleasure.

Oh, *man*…

James needed a distraction or he'd end up reliving parts of last night's rather memorable encounter and he'd already done that—more than once—this morning.

Every time he'd seen Sarah moving around the

barn as she got herself and Ivy ready for their trip into the medical centre.

For pretty much every minute of the long drive into work. Perhaps he should have taken his motorbike instead of Ella's car and that way he would have been forced to focus even more intently on the winding country road.

It had unexpectedly intruded on his thoughts once or twice in the debrief meeting that he would have normally been totally focused on, but that was because her name had been mentioned by others, including Cameron, who had come up to James at the end of the meeting to tell him he'd been very impressed with what he'd heard about Sarah. He'd asked him to pass on the message that if she was after a job in Aberdeen, they'd be more than happy to talk to her.

And it had taken his mind—and body—hostage when he'd stood at that bedroom door and realised that they could continue playing the game that Maureen had inadvertently started and pretend that they were Ivy's parents and in a relationship. That they were a couple who would be sharing the same bed…every single night…

The thought should have been enough to have James breaking out in a cold sweat but, instead, he was finding reassurance. The timeframe might be longer than he'd ever played with before but it still had a use-by date. Sarah had a home, friends and a job to go back to in Leeds. At some point in the not-too-distant future she would choose to return to her own life and everything would change again.

Rules could be rewritten. Or reinstated?

Okay, he'd made the suggestion that he could consider moving to Leeds in order to be part of Ivy's life, but it would be years before he could move that far away from his family. For heaven's sake, Mick would be arriving back very soon and helping to provide the support for his brother was the reason he had come here at all.

James pushed a speed dial button on his Bluetooth phone menu.

'Hey, bro. You haven't lost your telepathic abilities,' Eddie said. 'I was about to call you. Yesterday was a bit of a one-off, wasn't it?'

'Let's hope so.'

'How's that girl doing, do you know? Mika? The one with the crush injury. You stayed with her after we got her to Queen's, didn't you?'

'Until she went into Theatre, anyway. I've been up to visit her today. She's in an induced coma in ICU at the moment.'

'What's her renal function like?'

'Improving.'

'Potassium levels?'

'Under control.'

'She's lucky to have survived,' Eddie said.

'And that was only because Sarah was brave enough to crawl in there and start treating her. We would have had to lift the weight to get near her, and that could well have been fatal. She's quite something, isn't she?'

'Aye…' And not just professionally. Eddie had no idea…

'Mind you, she could only do what she was doing because you were handing her everything and calibrating the drugs and so on,' Eddie added. 'You made a good team.'

'We did…'

'I like her.' Eddie's statement was sincere.

'So do I.'

'She's not only brave, she's smart. And she's not bad-looking either.'

James made a noncommittal sound. He wasn't about to confess to his brother that he had got rather a lot closer to Sarah Harrison in the wake of their working together. In fact, he needed to change the subject.

'I've found a place to rent in town. Ferryhill. Not far from you and Jodie, in fact. I can move in before Ella and Logan get back. Possibly tomorrow if I can organise getting the lease agreement signed and utilities sorted.'

'That's great. Maybe we could combine a housewarming for you and a welcome home party for them. It would save us all trekking out to the countryside and it's much closer to the rehab centre for Mick. Did he tell you that he's going to be moved into one of the independent units when he gets back from New Zealand? He reckons he's going to be ready to find his own place soon. He's built up his upper body strength and is managing his own transfers really well now.'

'He told me that too. He sounds a lot happier, doesn't he?'

'Just as well. I was seriously worried about him for a while back there. I didn't think he was going to climb out of that hole.'

'I got the feeling that his physiotherapist had something to do with that. Have you noticed how often he talks about Riley?'

Eddie laughed. 'I asked him if he had some extra physical therapy going on there.'

'What did he say?'

'He was offended that I would cast aspersions on her professionalism. He's her patient, after all.'

James was laughing now. 'I seem to remember we didn't think she was overly professional telling him she wouldn't work with him if he didn't stop feeling sorry for himself.'

'I do think he fancies her. Maybe he's even fallen head over heels in love and he's just embarrassed that he wants to follow my example and try a grown-up relationship that involves serious commitment for a change.'

The idea was more than a little disturbing. Would that mean the vow the brothers had made years ago about living life to the full and never risking the kind of heartache that too often came with a long-term commitment or, worse, marriage was no longer even partially intact? That an excuse for the protective barrier James had always relied on no longer existed?

But this was about Mick, not himself.

'I almost hope he has,' he admitted quietly. 'I'd give anything to see him properly happy again.'

'He did sound a lot more positive.' Eddie's tone was thoughtful. 'He said he's got a surprise for us too, but he wouldn't tell me what it was. Do you think he might be bringing Riley back with him?'

James was pulling into the hospital car park. 'I don't think she'd be coming to the other side of the world after knowing someone for just a few weeks. Nobody falls in love that quickly, do they?' He didn't give Eddie a chance to respond. 'Gotta go, but I'll call you later. We'll plan that party.'

'Onto it. Oh, hey…?'

'What?'

'Sarah's not planning to go back to Leeds before we have a chance to have the party, is she? I know Ella's desperate to meet Ivy as soon as possible.'

'She'll be here. That's why I'm renting a house and not moving into your old apartment. There's room for all of us.'

'You're moving in together?' Eddie sounded astonished. 'That's fast work, even for you, mate.'

'Not like that,' James said. He could hear the offended tone in his own voice. 'It just made sense for Sarah to stay in Aberdeen a bit longer so we can work things out.'

'And you do seem to be managing to be in the same house without it being a problem.'

'Mmm.' The sound James made was a little strangled. Because he was remembering that master bedroom in the house they were about to move into?

Remembering how he'd looked at that bed and imagined being in there with Sarah?

Remembering the look in Sarah's eyes when, for some reason, he'd felt compelled to turn his head and catch her gaze?

She was just as interested in it happening again as he was, wasn't she?

Whether or not it *should* happen again, however, was a very different matter.

CHAPTER TEN

IT FELT DIFFERENT.

It might only be for a limited period of time but they were about to deliberately start living together. Up until now, they had simply been thrown together by fate and had both been guests in someone else's house.

They had chosen this house. Together.

It almost felt like…they were a couple…?

As if they hadn't stepped out of the pretence they'd gone along with when Maureen, the estate agent, had made that assumption about them.

Except there was more to it than that.

This was also about what had happened the night before they had been shown around this house. The sex.

That closeness that had hung in the air between them ever since, even though the sex hadn't happened again.

Had that been because James had had two afternoon shifts in a row that hadn't finished until midnight and Sarah wasn't going to stay up and make it look like she was waiting for him to come home?

Waiting for it to happen again when he might be perfectly justified in assuming it was the kind of one-off casual encounter that he was used to in his playboy lifestyle? The lifestyle that Sarah had informed him, in no uncertain terms during that first meeting, that she disapproved of so much? Okay…maybe he *had* been thinking about it when he'd given her that look in the master bedroom of this new house they would be sharing, but that didn't mean he had any intention of repeating it. And Sarah wasn't about to risk a polite rejection—or, worse, humiliation—by being the first to suggest that they should.

Sarah wasn't even sure she wanted it to happen again. Why ruin a memory that she could appreciate for the rest of her life when a second time couldn't possibly be as good? Added to that was a nagging wariness that she couldn't afford to ignore. There was a risk in doing something that could undermine a relationship between herself and James that was only just forming but needed to be rock solid as soon as possible. Not for herself so much, but for Ivy.

Thankfully, it had been such a busy couple of days it was surprisingly easy to not think about it much, as Sarah tackled housework and shopping and laundry in any spare moments that Ivy wasn't needing her attention. She wanted Ella and Logan to come home to find everything sparkling, the pantry restocked and fresh linen on the beds.

There was far more to sort and pack than she'd stuffed into her car for the journey up here to find Ivy's father and it took two trips into the city after the boxes of extra clothing and personal items sent up from Leeds arrived. How on earth had they managed to collect so much baby paraphernalia in such a short space of time?

It was a continuing process as well, it seemed.

A delivery truck pulled up in front of the house as she walked outside to put the last flattened box into the recycle bin after Ivy had gone down for her first afternoon nap in her new bedroom. When she turned back, she saw a top-of-the-range pram that must have cost a small fortune being wheeled towards her.

James appeared in the doorway and reached to sign for the delivery. 'I went shopping yesterday morning before work,' he explained. 'I thought it would be useful for all the walking that Maureen was talking about. In the park and along the river.'

Sarah discovered another item inside the pram when she parked it in the hallway under the coat rack that had James's leather bike jacket hanging from one of the hooks.

'It's called a baby bubble.' James held up the small, caterpillar-shaped padded sleeping bag with a hood. 'It's wind and rain proof. Because… you know…this is Scotland…'

The baby bubble had faux fur edging on the hood and fluffy ears on the top and it was so cute that Sarah felt strangely close to tears. She blinked hard but one of them escaped.

'Hey…what's up?' James dropped the baby bubble back into the pram and stepped close enough to catch that tear with his thumb. 'You don't like the baby bubble?'

'I love it,' Sarah said. 'And… I love that you chose this for Ivy.'

'She's my daughter.' The statement was matter-of-fact. 'I'll always do whatever I can to support her. And you…' James was still touching Sarah's face. 'If it wasn't for you, I wouldn't have known Ivy existed. And don't forget that I need you…'

He was talking about needing her to stay here to give him time to get used to having father-hood thrown at him from nowhere. About Sarah being prepared to care for Ivy so that he could keep working while he was coming to terms with this huge change in his life.

But…it felt as if he could be saying that he needed Sarah in a very different way…

And maybe he was? His fingers were threading themselves through her hair. Moving to cup her head the way they had the first time he had kissed her? She could feel a tension that was almost reluctance, though.

'We shouldn't be making this any more complicated than it already is,' James said quietly.

Sarah was losing her own battle to keep her eyes open and not let herself sink into this cloud of desire. She was trying to think of what Karly would say, which wasn't easy when something deep inside her body was melting and in this moment she wanted this man's touch more than anything on earth.

'It doesn't have to be complicated,' she whispered. 'It's just…'

The word for exactly what it was escaped her. She couldn't say it was just sex. Because this was James and he was Ivy's father and he had earned her respect despite anything she'd judged him on before she'd met him and…and she liked him. A lot.

James was staring at her and…she couldn't look away.

'Nice…' she finally said—in the heartbeat before James kissed her.

'Aye…nice,' he echoed when the kiss was finally broken. 'But…'

Again, Sarah could sense what wasn't being said. Was he thinking about a worst-case sce-

nario with her falling madly in love with him
and expecting something he would never be able
to give her and it would end like an acrimonious
divorce—complete with a child custody battle?

That his wings would be clipped even more
than the weight of the responsibilities he felt
to both Ivy and his brother Mick had already
achieved? What was the other part of that vow
he'd made with his brothers about never getting
trapped in something as confining as a marriage? Ah, yes…

'This is just about where we are right now,'
she reminded him. 'About living life. It won't
change anything. Ivy comes first, for both of us.
She always will. I promise…'

He knew she'd made a promise to Karly that
she would never break. And one to Ivy that
was going to last a lifetime. Sarah knew that he
would trust this promise being made to him now.
And why wouldn't he? She believed it herself.

She could feel that trust as he kissed her again.
As the heat got dialled up to a cell-scorching
level.

This time, if Ivy's nap continued for just a little bit longer, there would be no turning back,
for either of them.

'Nice' wasn't exactly the word James would have
chosen to describe the intoxicating delights of

snatching some very intimate time with Sarah, along with the solid friendship they seemed to be building, but it was definitely a good word for some of the changes he was currently getting used to.

It was nice to feel more in control of his own life, having signed the lease on this house with an option to renew in six months' time if he still had a job in Aberdeen and the owner of the house didn't decide to put it on the market.

It was nice to be living close to Eddie and Jodie and for it to be so easy to get to and from work. He could walk there and save parking hassles when he got around to selling his motorbike and purchasing a far more baby-friendly vehicle.

And this garden might not be as spectacular as the flowing lawns and duck pond at the barn conversion but it was still very...nice.

The swing wasn't the only bonus out here. There was a barbecue and pizza oven built out of bricks just outside the French doors that opened out from the kitchen. It made the whole ground floor, from the living room on the street side to the end of the private garden at the rear, an ideal entertainment area.

With a bit of furniture rearrangement and a portable, folding metal ramp that took care of the steps to the front door, it was also suitable for someone in a wheelchair to visit and the whole

Grisham family had gathered to celebrate the end of Ella and Logan's very belated honeymoon, Mick's homecoming, Eddie and Jodie moving in together and, most of all, to introduce Ivy to the other half of her father's family.

Eddie was in charge of steaks and sausages on the barbecue. James was about to start reheating pizzas in the wood-fired oven. Ella had finally given up cuddling the niece she had instantly fallen in love with to allow Uncle Mick to have a turn holding Ivy and Jodie and Sarah were clearly enjoying talking to each other. Logan was making it his mission to keep glasses topped up and look after the background music selection. There was laughter along with the music, the smell of good food and the warmth of being amongst family and it felt so *nice* that it was bringing a bit of a lump to James's throat, to be honest.

Because there had been so little to celebrate in what had brought the Grisham siblings together in recent times that James had felt more than a bit broken himself. It had been almost as bad as that dreadful period when they'd lost their mother to cancer when the triplets had only been teenagers. The worst time had been that awful period in Mick's early rehabilitation after his serious spinal injury when he'd become so depressed he'd completely stopped eating and was avoiding talking to anyone by pretending to be asleep when they visited.

Ella and Eddie—who'd already changed his entire life to move back to Scotland to support his brother—had thrown themselves into working with the rehabilitation centre's psychologists and therapists to support Mick and James had travelled up and down from Edinburgh too many times to count to spend as much time with his brother as he could. It was Ella and Logan who had discovered the rehabilitation centre in New Zealand that was gaining worldwide recognition in their successful treatment of spinal patients and they had hatched the plan of taking a belated honeymoon so that they could take Mick to spend some time at the centre.

It had clearly been the best idea they could have come up with.

Being needed for housesitting for Ella and Logan had brought James back into the heart of his family. And Mick was looking so much happier. Healthier. He sounded so positive as he talked about plans for his immediate future.

'I'm going to start driving lessons and I'll order an adapted car as soon as I get the hang of the hand controls for braking and accelerating. I can already transfer myself in and out of a car to my chair.'

The surprise Mick had been saving to show them was the movement he now had in his feet.

'I'm getting sensation back in my legs too. They're warning me that it might not be enough to get me walking again, but they have no idea how hard I'm going to work on it. One day— soon, I hope—I intend to walk back into that centre in New Zealand and show Riley just how far I've come. And how proud she can be of the job *she* does.'

James and Eddie had shared a glance. Not that they were counting, but it did seem like Riley's name was being dropped into the conversation at very frequent intervals.

'I'm going to start looking for a place of my own too. It's time I got out of rehab. And I'm taking up swimming. It was Riley that got me started. She even got me out in the ocean before I left. How awesome is that? I never thought I'd feel waves on my skin again.'

James swallowed the lump in his throat that had grown to the point of being painful. 'How 'bout handing my daughter back to her mum so she can put her down to sleep? Dinner's ready…'

Her mum…

It sounded as if James really thought of her as Ivy's mother, which made the bond between them as her parents seem more real, somehow. Deeper.

It made Sarah a part of this amazing family as well. She'd already met Eddie and Jodie and knew that a true friendship with them both was going to be easy, but the triplets' big sister Ella was irresistible.

'I adore babies,' she'd told Sarah. 'I'm going to be the perfect auntie for this precious wee dot. You just tell me whatever I can do to help...' She pressed a hand to her heart. 'That *hair*... It brings back so many memories.'

'I've seen the photo of the triplets when they were babies. I've heard the story about the hair-cutting incident too.'

'Oh, there are plenty more stories, believe me...' Ella was laughing. 'I thought I would be put off having a baby of my own for ever after helping raise the "Fearsome Threesome", but after a cuddle with wee Ivy...' She looked up, her gaze going straight to her husband, whose head turned as if he had felt a touch. 'You never know, do you? Even at my age...'

Mick was reluctant to give Ivy back to Sarah.

'I think she likes me,' he said with a grin. 'And I think I like being an uncle. I've never been one before. I need to practise.'

Oh, these Grisham brothers certainly knew how to charm women. Even the tiniest of them had succumbed, judging by that half smile on Ivy's face as she trustingly drifted towards sleep.

'You're not hungry?'

'It'll take James and Eddie a while to get that food on the table. Look—they're arguing about how well those sausages are cooked now.'

Sure enough, Sarah could see James shaking his head sadly as he pointed to a sausage, but both he and Eddie were laughing and even Mick, too far away to be a part of whatever the joke was, was chuckling.

It was strange to be in a room with all the triplets. The three brothers weren't identical but they were similar enough in their looks to all be extremely attractive men with their height and build and that matching dark hair and eyes. There was an edge to Mick that suggested he might well have been the ringleader in their mischief as children and Sarah suspected James was correct in his memory that it had been Mick who'd stolen the nail scissors and initiated that famous haircutting incident.

Ivy stirred and made a sound. It looked as though she was trying to find a more comfortable position in Mick's arms.

'I should put her into her bassinet for a nap,' Sarah said. 'Otherwise, she could get grumpy and you might get put off being an uncle.'

'Swap you for my phone then,' Mick said. 'I left it on the table over there.'

When Sarah handed Mick his phone she must have touched a side button enough for the screen to light up and reveal the image that had been saved as the locked screen wallpaper. Mick must have taken it as a selfie, but he wasn't alone. A woman with bouncy blonde hair and the happiest smile ever was tilting her head far enough sideways to touch his and be in the centre of the photo.

Sarah caught her bottom lip between her teeth. 'Is that Riley?'

He didn't need to respond. She could see it in his eyes—along with so much more—as she handed him the phone and lifted Ivy from the crook of his elbow. She could sense just how much Mick was in love with this woman who was now on the other side of the world to where he was. Instinct also told Sarah that she could well be the only other person who knew and that Mick would prefer it to stay a secret between them. Was that because of that vow the brothers had made years ago—on his behalf, in fact—to not risk the kind of heartbreak Mick had already experienced when he got jilted?

But her heart still ached for Mick as she carried Ivy upstairs, because it was quite possible that his feelings had been secret all along and he hadn't been able to get anywhere near as close to Riley as he'd wanted to be. How easy would it be to fall in love with someone who had been supporting him and encouraging him to believe in himself as he battled such a huge physical challenge? But how impossible would it have been for Riley to allow anything too personal to develop between herself and her patient? It must have felt like a hopeless crush as far as Mick was concerned.

When she came back downstairs, James and Eddie had sorted the meat and pizzas and the dining room table was covered with platters of hot food, fresh bread and salads. Mick was making a joke about the bonus of being in a wheelchair at a buffet because he didn't have to find anywhere to sit down and eat.

Sarah found herself quietly watching all the interactions within this family, with the buzz of animated conversation and plates of food being topped up and enjoyed. If Sarah's stumbling on the secret of what Mick might be feeling about Riley had made things more difficult for him, he wasn't showing it, but both Eddie and James were right beside him and they wanted to hear more about his stay in one of the most beautiful places in New Zealand. They also wanted to hear about all the places Ella and Logan had gone on their camper van tour. There was a lot of teasing and bursts of laughter and just the way everybody looked at each other or offered a touch or quick hug made the unbreakable bonds between these people very obvious, and it was particularly powerful between these triplet brothers.

There was so much love in this room.

This was Ivy's family. And Sarah was being welcomed as part of it.

As Ivy's mum.

This was so much bigger than the feeling of being a co-parent with James. Or the other half of a couple, even. This was the kind of love Sarah had dreamed of finding and it was filling her heart to the point it felt like she didn't have room to take a breath. Her gaze drifted to where James was deep in conversation with Mick and she could feel her whole body softening as she looked at him.

The feeling of that love was still there, but suddenly it had a much sharper focus. A spear of sensation that was threatening to crack her heart open.

Oh…dear *Lord*…

So much for pretending she could be like Karly and be able to have a casual sexual relationship with an impossibly gorgeous playboy and then walk away from it, unscathed, to carry on with her own life. She was in very real danger of falling in love with James Grisham, wasn't she?

She had broken her promise.

No… Sarah managed to drag her gaze away from James. What she had promised was that Ivy would always come first and nothing would be allowed to change that. She put her plate down on the table and headed towards the hallway and the stairs—as if she'd heard a whimper from Ivy's direction.

She could control this. Nip it in the bud before it went any further because she was only just aware of the possibility of falling. If Mick had been able to keep how he felt about Riley a secret when he had already fallen, she could do the same with James even more easily because it hadn't happened yet. She could step back from the brink. If he didn't know, nothing needed to change.

And Sarah didn't want anything to change.

Because she didn't want to lose this glimpse of a life that was everything she could have wished. This was the ultimate dream of family that she and Karly had both missed out on but had tried to create for each other. And this was about putting Ivy first.

The sudden overwhelmingly strong realisation that hit Sarah in that moment made her turn back to let her gaze sweep over the whole group of people that had gathered in this room this evening.

This was where Ivy belonged.

With her father and extended family, who already loved her.

There was no way Sarah could justify taking her back to Leeds.

But there was also no way she could stay unless she could keep how she felt about James a complete and utter secret.

And not go even a single step closer to that brink.

CHAPTER ELEVEN

A WEEK LATER and counting and Sarah was pretty sure she was winning.

She'd just needed to recognise what was needed for her own health and wellbeing and put plans of action and any necessary barriers into place.

Routines had been a part of Sarah's life for as long as she could remember, after all. Eating the right food at the right time. Checking her blood glucose levels and calculating the amount of insulin she needed to inject. Exercising regularly and keeping herself as healthy as possible. The predictability of her routines represented both an insurance policy and a safety net and allowed her to feel like she had control, despite the curve balls life had a habit of throwing.

Even the unexpected and rather large balls that had just come in Sarah's direction, of moving to a new house, realising that she might never return to the place she'd grown up in and—almost—falling in love with someone who had told her that he'd actually made a vow with his brothers that he would never marry. Or get 'caught' in a permanent relationship.

These last months—since Karly had confessed she was pregnant, in fact—had seen the biggest challenges Sarah had ever faced to hang onto her old routines when she had to build new ones around them. She'd come scarily close to failing, when she was struggling with the grief of Karly dying and that night she'd had the hypoglycaemic crisis in front of James. But, looking back, Sarah could already see that she had learned to adapt and there was a new confidence to be found in having coped with such major changes in her life. A confidence that she'd already been able to use to good effect on the day of that disaster scene response.

She had needed some more of that confidence since the move into this lovely old house in Ferryhill too. Or, rather, since she'd recognised the danger she was in, of getting her heart broken by letting herself fall in love with James Grisham. The change in lifestyle was not proving difficult at all. Right from that night when they'd hosted the family gathering, new routines were emerging and…

And Sarah was loving them.

Early mornings were almost the same, except that Ivy now had her own room between Sarah's and the master bedroom that she'd insisted James used because, after all, this was *his* house. The kitchen, which caught the earliest rays of sunlight, was the perfect place to sit and feed Ivy and Sarah could enjoy the peanut butter toast and a mug of tea that had been her favourite breakfast since she was twelve years old.

Later in the mornings, Sarah would put Ivy into the pram James had surprised her with the day they'd moved in and she would walk—through the park and along the river, sometimes taking a sandwich and some fruit to sit and have a picnic lunch somewhere. The local shops were within easy walking distance to get fresh vegetables and other ingredients for dinner and she'd seen notices on a community board advertising local playgroups and events.

The lifestyle was almost as much of a fantasy as real life could deliver, in fact. Sarah was living in what could be a perfect place to bring up a child. In a perfect house. And the element that was straight out of a fantasy she had never even considered playing with, living with a man who seemed only too happy to make her nights as perfect as everything else.

And, yes, of course she knew life wasn't going to last quite like this for ever but, because she knew that, it was okay to make the most of it while it did last, wasn't it? Because it was making it so much easier to make the big decisions about what came next.

The thought that she couldn't take Ivy too far away from her biological family had not changed. If anything, it had embedded itself firmly enough for her to broach the subject with James during dinner one night when they were well and truly settled in to the new house.

'Is there any chance of your locum position here becoming permanent?'

James gave her a startled glance. 'Were you talking to someone when you came in to visit Mika today? Someone like Cameron?'

'I did see Cameron in ICU but we weren't talking about you. Why? Has he said something?'

James shook his head. 'Maybe you're telepathic. He asked me the same question this morning. Said it seems likely that the person I'm covering isn't coming back.' He raised an eyebrow. 'What *were* you talking about?'

'Mika. He'd come up to see how she was doing after her latest surgery yesterday.'

They had both been closely following the progress of the outdoor education student they'd been so involved in rescuing on the day of the viewing platform collapse and the mention of Mika's name had distracted James from the question she'd asked.

'How *is* she?'

'Amazingly positive, even though it's still not certain she's going to keep that leg.'

'I'm keeping my fingers crossed that she won't end up being a double amputee.'

'I think she'd still do well. She's a remark-able young woman,' Sarah said. 'She's got a long road ahead of her but she's got an amazing level of courage and determination and she's lucky enough to have a close family around her. Like Mick is to have all of you. He's doing astonish-ingly well, isn't he?'

'He sure is. I've never seen him quite this de-termined. But he's got a way to go yet.'

'That's why I asked about your job. You'd want to stay here if you could, wouldn't you? To support Mick?'

James put down his fork as if his appetite had just vanished. 'I'd want to be as close as possi-ble,' he said quietly. 'Of course I would. But I don't want to be too far away from Ivy either. It's very important to me that I'm a meaningful part of her life.'

'I know...' Sarah took a deep breath. 'That's why I'm thinking that maybe I should move here. To Aberdeen. I don't want Ivy to miss out on having a family like yours around her. It's something I never had and I always knew there was something huge missing from my life.'

James was staring at her. 'You'd do that? What about your friends? And your job?'

'Didn't you tell me that Cameron said he'd be happy to talk to me about applying for a job at Queen's if I ever wanted one?'

'After that major incident? Aye…he did say that but…you'd be starting a whole new life here and…that's a big deal. Are you really considering it?'

Sarah could feel her lips curving a little. 'I started a whole new life the moment Ivy was born. No…it was more like the moment Karly told me she was pregnant. And it's not as if I'd be moving somewhere I didn't know anyone. I'm already making new friends. Jodie, for instance. And your sister, Ella.'

She could see that James was still trying to take in her suggestion. As if something about it was troubling him?

Oh…of course…

'I'd find my own place,' she assured him. 'I wouldn't expect to keep living with *you*.' Sarah's smile widened. She even gave a huff of laughter. 'It would cramp your style a bit, wouldn't it? You'd never be able to bring a date home.' She picked up her plate to carry to the kitchen bench because she'd lost her appetite as well. 'We both need our own lives,' she said as she stood up. 'But Ivy can grow up knowing how important she is to both of us. To all of us. I promised Karly I'd do everything I could to look after Ivy, and giving her a whole family to help protect and raise her is...' Sarah had to swallow hard. 'It's so much more than I could ever give her by myself so it's a no-brainer. It's the right thing to do.'

James was standing up as well. He looked as if he might have a bit of a lump in his own throat. He didn't say anything but he didn't need to. Because he came and took the plate out of Sarah's hands and put it down on the table again. And then he wrapped his arms around her and hugged her.

So tightly it was hard to breathe, but Sarah didn't mind.

Because this was telling her how much of a gift this would be for James, as well as his beloved family.

And...it felt like love...

It had just been a throwaway sort of comment about needing to find her own place so that she didn't cramp James's style.

A joke, even?

But it came back to bite Sarah. Hard.

While the kitchen end of the house caught the first rays of sun, it was the living room that got any late afternoon warmth and it was particularly welcome after a day of caring for a baby who seemed a little off-colour. Ivy hadn't settled for her usual sleep periods, which was unlike her enough to have already increased Sarah's anxiety levels.

'What's the matter, Button?' The bottle of milk was less than half empty but Ivy had lost interest and looked like she might fall asleep at any moment. 'Are you just tired because you haven't had a proper nap yet today?' She dropped a kiss onto the soft spikes of Ivy's hair. 'Let's put you to bed and see if that helps.'

Ivy seemed happy enough to be put into her bassinet and Sarah came back downstairs, turning to glance out of the bay window at the front of the house as she went into the living room on her way to the kitchen. It had become a habit to enjoy a glimpse of the bricked path to the gate and the street beyond with its lovely leafy trees.

She noticed she had left Ivy's cute fluffy lamb lovey on the window seat so she picked it up along with the half empty bottle of milk, looking out of the window again as she straightened. Sometimes she stood here with Ivy in her arms, watching for James to arrive home on his motorbike. Stealing a moment to watch him take off his helmet and unfasten the leather jacket that he would hang on the coat rack as he came through the front door. Letting delicious tendrils of a physical attraction, that was showing no signs of wearing off, weave their way through her entire body.

She hadn't expected him to arrive home this early today, however. And, even more strangely, to be in a taxi that was pulling to a stop right in front of the gate? With remarkable clarity, Sarah found herself stepping back in time to when she'd first laid eyes on James Grisham as he'd stepped out of a taxi. But he didn't walk straight towards her this time. He didn't even know she was watching and she knew he wasn't even thinking about her. He was turning back to the taxi, clearly waiting for someone else to emerge.

Sarah couldn't help remembering who else had been in that taxi that night now. Janine—with her long blonde hair—hanging on his arm. Calling him 'Jimmy'. Pouting with disappointment because she wasn't going to be invited to go inside his sister's house.

Was she in *this* taxi?

About to be invited into *this* house?

It was a woman getting out. And she was blonde, but Sarah knew instantly that it wasn't Janine. It wasn't someone that James was dating either. To her amazement, Sarah recognised Riley—the gorgeous physiotherapist whose photo she'd seen on Mick's phone.

It should have been a relief.

A joyous moment, even, because the only reason that Riley might have to turn up in Aberdeen would be to see Mick, and surely she wouldn't have travelled right across the globe to do that unless she was missing him?

As much as he was missing her?

James was smiling as if he knew he was helping to deliver a fairy tale ending for his brother, but all Sarah could think of was how she'd felt when she'd expected to see Janine getting out of that taxi.

As if the bottom of her world was about to fall out.

As if her heart was about to break into a million pieces.

Had she really believed she had halted the process of falling in love with James Grisham? That she could even joke about him dating women in the future and be okay about it?

She couldn't have been more wrong.

About everything.

Well, not about the dating. Of course he would go back to a lifestyle that was a big part of who he was. He had a vow to keep, didn't he? To live life to the full. To never get 'caught'. Seeing him with other women was going to be a part of her future if she was a part of his life. Possibly a never-ending stream of women and his intimate time with her would be nothing more than a pleasant, but distant, memory. Or perhaps he might even include her occasionally on a strictly 'friends with benefits' kind of arrangement?

She couldn't do that.

Because what she *had* been wrong about was thinking she had only been in danger of falling in love with James. It had already happened by the time the thought had even occurred to her, hadn't it? Maybe the crash landing had been disguised by the emotional overload of working with him during that rescue mission. Or buried under the astonishing revelation of how amazing it had been to go to bed with him. To have him make love to her…

Oh, help…

If she couldn't live with James being a significant part of her life but she also couldn't live with taking Ivy away from her real family, what was left?

Going back to Leeds alone…?

No…

That was unthinkable.

Sarah turned away from the window before Riley came through the gate and James followed with the large suitcase he had pulled out of the taxi. She rather wished she hadn't put Ivy to bed because she could really do with a cuddle right now.

She was in trouble. Part of her was desperately

trying to wrap something tightly enough around her heart to stop it breaking apart.

Pressing the lamb lovey over the top of her heart felt like it was helping to hold it together just a little. Sarah could even catch a waft of that gorgeous smell of baby. But it still felt like she was in trouble.

Big trouble...

CHAPTER TWELVE

'This is Riley, Sarah.' James put the suitcase down beside Ivy's pram. 'She was Mick's physio in New Zealand. I'm sure you've heard him talking about her. Riley, this is Sarah. Ivy's mum.'

'I recognise you from your photo on Mick's phone,' Sarah said. 'I'm so happy to meet you, Riley.'

Sarah was smiling but James could feel that something wasn't quite right.

'Sorry not to give you any warning,' he apologised. 'But it's been a bit full-on. I had no idea myself that Riley was coming here.'

'I'd only been talking to Ella,' Riley admitted, 'because I'd met her and Logan in New Zealand. I needed to try and find out how Mick might feel if I turned up.'

'I could have told you.' Sarah's smile still looked oddly forced. 'He's going to be *so* happy.'

Riley was smiling back. 'That's what Ella thought but…oh… I was so nervous about taking a risk this big. And then I thought…what the heck? It might end up being a disaster or I might end up with the love of my life but, either way, I had to come.' Her smile turned into a grimace, though. 'And then Ella wasn't there to meet me at the airport and, next thing I know, I hear my name being called—asking me to go urgently to the information desk.'

'Ella had a bit of a vagal turn and fainted,' James put in. 'She was being looked after by the airport medic. She was okay but she very sensibly got Riley to drive her back and called Logan, who insisted that she came into the ED to get checked.'

Sarah was looking quite pale herself now. 'Oh, my God... Is she okay?'

James nodded. 'Better than okay, if you ask me. Turns out she got pregnant while she was on her honeymoon and hadn't realised, what with everything else going on.' He grinned at Sarah. 'Piglet's going to get a wee cousin,' he said. 'How cool is that? Logan's still with her and they're getting an ultrasound. He said they'd call in on their way home and let us know the results.'

'I'd better put the kettle on.'

'Eddie and Jodie have gone to pick up Mick and bring him here as well.'

James was watching Sarah's face carefully and her expression reminded him of the first time he'd ever seen her, standing in the head-lights of that taxi. Frozen.

Frightened…?

Lost…?

He needed to touch her. To try and let her know that she had nothing to worry about. Not if he was by her side.

'Sorry…' James stepped close enough to Sarah for their arms to touch. 'It comes with trip-let territory. You know— If something happens to one of us, it kind of happens to all of us— good or bad. With Riley here and Ella's news, this is definitely one of the good life-changing days that need celebrating.'

'It is…' Was it his imagination or was Sarah shrinking away from his touch? 'It's not a prob-lem. It's what families do. It's a good thing…'

She was avoiding eye contact with him. Mov-ing so that there was a physical space between them as well. For some reason, Riley's arrival seemed to have rattled Sarah, and James had no idea why. Or perhaps it was the idea of his whole family arriving en masse, without any of the planning that had gone into the last family party? She'd been rather quiet later on during that evening, come to think of it, although no-body else would have noticed. But then, nobody knew Sarah as well as James did…

He knew that something had changed.

Something big.

He just didn't know what until about an hour later, when the whole clan had gathered. Ella and Logan had arrived first, radiating the joy of their news, and they'd hatched a plan for Riley to be sitting on the window seat in the living area and Eddie and Jodie would bring Mick in and then keep walking to the other end of the house and out into the garden to where the rest of the family would be, so that Mick and Riley's reunion would be as private as possible.

James texted the plan to Eddie. 'Let's hope Ivy doesn't wake up and spoil the moment.'

'I think she'll be sleeping for a while,' Sarah said. 'She's been a bit unsettled today.'

Ivy did stay asleep. Eddie and Jodie played their part of the plan and when, some time later, Mick wheeled himself into the kitchen with Riley on his lap, her arms around his neck and tears of happiness streaking her cheeks, it was very obvious that this was a happy ending happening right in front of them. The way they were looking at each other had the kind of emotional kick that was there in every glance between Ella and Logan, especially after the surprise they'd had today. Between Eddie and Jodie as well, now that he was so aware of it.

It was the look of love.

The kind of passionate love that James would

never experience for himself but was all he wanted for the people he already loved so much so it was kind of contagious. His smile felt misty and he wanted to share his own happiness so he sought out Sarah's gaze.

And then it hit him, like a ton of bricks.

Because Sarah was looking at him the way all his siblings were looking at their partners.

With that level of love that went so far beyond friendship it... Well, it felt as if the axis of James's world was suddenly tilted. It was blindsiding because this wasn't supposed to have happened. Sarah had promised that getting as close as they had wasn't going to change anything. That it wouldn't be a problem to give in to their attraction to each other because it wasn't a big deal. She knew he didn't do significant relationships. She knew it was only temporary.

But it had clearly already gone on too long and it had to stop before it went any further.

Before Sarah got badly hurt.

Or Ivy...

It was hard, being in this group of people who were all *so* happy.

But it was even worse when they all left far too soon because they all wanted to be alone with each other.

That left Sarah alone with James as the door

closed after Eddie and Jodie had driven away, after juggling a suitcase and wheelchair into their vehicle, to take Riley back to Mick's unit.

And a silence that was deep enough to drown in suddenly filled the space between them in the hallway.

Somehow, James knew that this pretence of playing happy families themselves was over just as much as Sarah did, didn't he?

All it needed was for someone to say something and Sarah found she was brave enough to be the one to do that.

For Ivy's sake.

'I can't live here with you any longer, James,' she said, very quietly.

'I know.'

There was a catch in James's voice that told Sarah he knew why she couldn't stay, and that was…heartbreaking, because he wasn't going to try and stop her, was he? The longer they kept living in the same house, the more of a problem this was going to become and that wouldn't be fair on any of them. Including Ivy.

Especially Ivy…

'Where will you go?'

'I don't know.' Sarah couldn't meet his gaze.

'You don't need to go anywhere just yet,' James said. 'Eddie hasn't found anyone to take over his old apartment. I could stay there and give you a bit of time to look for something?'

'I should probably go back to Leeds.' Sarah forced the words out. 'There are things that need sorting there so that I can make new decisions. Like my flat.'

And her job.

And the rest of her life?

James was nodding but he didn't say anything for a long moment. A moment that was long enough for them both to feel that silence again. For them both to feel the horror of the sound that suddenly came from the top of the stairs. A cry like no other that Ivy had ever made in her life so far.

It was a scream of pain. So shrill and heart-rending it cut through Sarah like a knife. She saw her own shock reflected in James's eyes for the split second before they both turned to get up the stairs as fast as humanly possible.

Ivy was still making that strange cry as they went into her bedroom.

'It's abdo pain.' James was standing back, as if he was in front of a tiny patient who'd been brought into his emergency department and was trying to gather all the information he could, as quickly as he could. 'Look at the way she's drawing her legs up like that. And she's very pale.'

Sarah couldn't stand back. She was reaching

to pick Ivy up and comfort her. She held Ivy close, making soothing sounds and rocking her gently as if she might be able to suck some of that pain into her own body and make things better. And maybe it did, because the high-pitched crying stopped almost as suddenly as it had started.

James still sounded like a doctor. 'You said she was unsettled today?'

'She just wasn't herself. And she wasn't very hungry.' Sarah pressed her cheek against Ivy's. 'I don't think she's running a temperature. Is it colic?'

'I don't know,' James said. 'Can you put her down on the bed for a minute? I'd like to check her tummy. And her nappy.'

Ivy screamed again when she felt even gentle pressure on her abdomen. It was Sarah who discovered the blood in her nappy and it was then that she realised they had both stepped into a nightmare that wasn't going to end any time soon because it was just beginning. She wanted to grab Ivy into her arms again and start running. To find safety. Somewhere…somehow… Panic was clawing at her until she felt James touch her, his hand on her arm, his gaze waiting to meet hers.

'It's okay, Sarah,' he said softly. 'We've got this. We're going to take Ivy into the hospital.'

* * *

It wasn't simply so much easier to be able to pull the cloak of professionalism around him to deal with every parent's nightmare.

It was the only way James could deal with this without falling apart.

Sarah was absolutely focused on Ivy. Holding her whenever she was allowed to. Glued to the side of the bed, stroking the baby's head and talking to her at other times, like when they had to get a cannula in to get a blood sample and start giving Ivy some antibiotics. She stayed right where she was and wore a lead apron when X-rays had to be taken.

James focused just as intently on the medical side of what was happening and what was being done and said around him.

'Heart rate's one-sixty. She's got a respiratory rate of thirty-six.'

That was okay. Normal.

'White cell count and CRP are normal. No signs of sepsis.'

'Lung fields are clear on X-ray, but look at this abdominal view... Looks like a soft tissue mass in the right iliac fossa...'

That wasn't okay. But James had suspected it would be the case.

'Let's get an ultrasound and get a paediatric surgical consult down here. Call Radiology too.

It's looking far more like an intussusception than gastro or sepsis.'

The ultrasound confirmed a diagnosis of an obstruction caused by one part of Ivy's bowel telescoping in on itself.

'We'll make up to three attempts of three minutes each to reduce the intussusception by air pressure under fluoroscopy,' the radiologist told James and Sarah. 'I should warn you that, in perhaps one in a hundred children, this procedure could cause or reveal a perforation that might get rapidly larger and, in that case, she'll need surgery to repair the hole. I'll get the consent forms for you to sign.'

Sarah was holding Ivy, who was, thankfully, now asleep thanks to the pain relief she had been given. Sarah was looking so pale James hoped she was keeping a very careful eye on her blood glucose levels but she didn't sound as if her level of alertness was diminished enough to be another symptom of hypoglycaemia. If anything, she was hyper-focused.

'Can I stay with her?' she asked quietly.

'I'll stay with her,' James said quickly, because he knew that Sarah's request would be denied but, as a medic here himself, he was confident his colleagues wouldn't prevent him being present. 'But you won't have to wait alone.' He tilted his head and Sarah turned swiftly to see

Mick wheeling his chair towards where they were standing in the corridor. Eddie was walking beside him.

Sarah blinked. 'How did they know…?'

James shrugged. This sort of thing had happened more than once in their lifetimes. 'Eddie texted when Ivy was having the ultrasound to ask if everything was okay. I had to tell him what was going on.'

And now his brothers were here to support him and they could do that by supporting Sarah while she had to wait. He held out his arms but avoided meeting Sarah's gaze directly because he didn't want to see the fear he knew would be there.

'I'll take Ivy now,' he said.

The baby woke up as she was moved and began crying again but James didn't falter. He simply turned and walked away.

Sarah could still hear Ivy's cries even when she was well out of earshot, in a comfortable family room with Mick and Eddie.

She was way too close to crying herself. Maybe distraction would help?

'Has the jet lag hit Riley yet?'

'Sure has. I made her a cup of tea and by the time I took it to her she was out like a light on the couch. I just covered her up with a blanket when Eddie came to get me. Jodie said she'd stay there so we didn't have to wake her up.'

'I still don't get how you knew something was wrong.'

'It just happens,' Mick said. 'It's a multiple sibling thing, I think. Like twins often have.'

Sarah bit her lip. Distraction wasn't helping.

'It's going to be all right,' Eddie added. 'These guys do this kind of thing all the time and they're good. Jimmy won't let anything happen to Ivy.'

Those tears were closer as Sarah remembered the rigid lines of James's back as he'd walked away carrying Ivy.

'He just walked away,' she whispered. 'With Ivy in his arms. He didn't even look back.'

Eddie and Mick exchanged a glance. Eddie shook his head and Mick swivelled his wheelchair so that he was right beside where Sarah was perched on the edge of a small sofa. Close enough to put his hand on her arm.

'That's just James,' he said. 'Sometimes the way he copes is by putting up a wall and hiding behind it. It's not because of anything you did.'

But Sarah couldn't accept the comfort. James hadn't even looked at her when he'd taken Ivy from her arms. It was hard to breathe past the tightness in her chest and she could feel her eyes beginning to fill. 'I told him tonight that

I couldn't live with him any longer,' she confessed. 'I think he already knew why.'

Eddie crouched in front of her. 'What are you talking about?' he asked. 'What did he know?'

'That I broke the rules…' There was no stopping the tears now. 'I fell in love with him.'

It was Mick who got the box of tissues from the table and handed handfuls to Sarah. It was Eddie who rubbed her back.

'It's not that he doesn't care,' he said. 'It's probably because he cares too much.'

Sarah looked up. 'What do you mean?'

It was Mick who answered her. 'I don't know if he told you, but we lost our mum to cancer when we were still at high school. Ella was away at university by then and, while she came home as often as possible, she wasn't there all the time. Jimmy was the hardest hit of all of us and that was partly because he was always the sensitive one out of the three of us. He had to try and make us feel better. It didn't matter how bad he was feeling himself.'

Eddie was nodding. 'Losing Mum—and then Dad, not long after that—was devastating for him. That was when he started building that wall. And he used it a lot, especially when we started dating. He always made sure he didn't get in too deep. He had us. We had him. We didn't need anyone else.'

'Until we did,' Mick said ruefully. 'But then there was Juliana and I said I was never getting anywhere near getting married again.'

'And we all made that stupid pact.' Eddie shook his head. 'All I can say is that I couldn't be happier that I've broken it.'

'I reckon you all know I've broken it now too…' Mick was touching Sarah's arm again. 'And I think Jimmy knows what he's been lucky enough to find. It might just take him a bit of time to come out from behind that damn wall.'

'We've seen you together,' Eddie added. 'You and James and Ivy. You're already a family…'

Thank goodness his family was there to keep Sarah company.

James had felt that distance increasing with every step he had taken away from Sarah with Ivy in his arms. He knew how hard the waiting would be for her when she had no idea what was actually happening or how long it might take.

But it wasn't easy being in this room either. Far from it.

He'd been allowed in because he was a part of the medical community in this hospital and this patient was his daughter, but maybe that would have been a good reason to have kept him out?

He knew too much, didn't he?

He was standing to one side of this room, trying to focus on what everybody could see on the fluoroscopy screens as the air pressure was gradually increased, but it was nothing more than a blur as his thoughts spiralled.

What if the radiologist's warning had been well founded and there *was* already a perforation in her bowel that had been missed? Or the pressure was enough to create one?

What if they rushed her into emergency surgery but it was already too late to stop the infection and it developed into peritonitis and then septic shock as her tiny body summoned an overwhelming immune system response to the infection?

What if her blood pressure dropped so low it could lead to a dramatic failure of vital organs like her lungs and kidneys and liver and it would be impossible to fight hard enough to save Ivy's life?

However tiny that risk was, it was enough for James to find himself confronting the unthinkable possibility that he could lose Ivy.

It was creating a pain that felt as if his heart was cracking wide open.

And James knew exactly what created that particular pain.

Love…

He loved Ivy. This wasn't just about parental responsibility or the connection of shared DNA or how proud he was of his daughter. It wasn't even anything to do with how adorable this particular baby was and how good it could make him feel to cuddle her or see her smile.

This was true love. As big as the love James had for the brothers who were such a part of who he was himself. For his adored big sister who'd been another mum. And, of course, for his beloved mother he still missed every day.

Those cracks in his heart were getting so wide he could fall into them. If he lost Ivy, he'd lose Sarah as well.

But he was going to lose her anyway, wasn't he?

'I can't live here with you any longer, James...'

And now he could see that look in her eyes. The look that told him how much she loved him. He wanted that love.

He needed it.

As much as he needed the oxygen he was pulling into his lungs through the mask he was wearing.

Because he felt the same way.

'James?' The radiologist sounded as if he was repeating his name. 'Can you see that? We just need to finish up but it's a total success, first go. We'll have to keep an eye on her overnight to make sure it doesn't revert but we're all done.'

No...

Ivy might be fine and would be ready to be taken to the paediatric observation ward very soon, but they weren't all done. Not by a long shot.

'I'll be right back,' he said.

'Sarah? Can you come out here for a sec?'

'What is it, Mick?' Sarah got to her feet in a hurry.

'Maybe the vending machine down the hall isn't working.' Eddie followed Sarah out of the relatives' room.

But this had nothing to do with the vending machine Mick had gone to investigate. They could all see James walking towards them. Eddie and Mick shared a glance and then a smile and simply melted away into the background so Sarah was standing by herself as James got closer.

He wasn't avoiding her gaze this time. He was holding on to it. Or was it Sarah who was clinging to his?

'Is she…? Is Ivy…?'

'She's fine.'

Oh, *my*… Were those *tears* in his eyes? From relief? Had he been as scared as Sarah had been about losing Ivy?

Except… James was smiling at the same time. At her. And it looked exactly like that hug had felt that day. When she'd said she would stay in Aberdeen so that Ivy could be with her whole family. When he'd hugged her so tightly it had been too hard to breathe but it didn't matter.

Because it felt like love…

And James was holding out his hand to her.

'Come with me,' he said softly. 'Ivy needs her mum.' He took hold her of her hand and she could feel that love through his skin, rushing into her body to find her heart. He gave it a little squeeze as if he wanted to emphasise his words.

'She loves you so much,' he added softly. 'And so do I.'

'I love you too.'

Nothing more needed to be said in this moment. There would be plenty of time to say it all later. To share how astonishing it was to have fallen in love with both a baby and her father. For now, Sarah just held the hand of this man she loved with all her heart and they walked away together.

To be with their daughter…

EPILOGUE

Four years later...

THEY STOOD, shoulder to shoulder, in matching tuxedos at the front of the church.

Three men.

Three brothers.

James, Edward and Michael Grisham.

There'd never been any doubt that they would be together in such a significant moment in all their lives when Mick was finally going to marry the love of his life in this beautiful old stone church on the outskirts of Aberdeen, Scotland.

The brothers were smiling at each other.

'Déjà vu,' James murmured. 'It's not the first time we all stood in front of an altar like this.'

Mick raised an eyebrow. 'It might not be the first, but it will definitely be the last. And if either of you had waited a bit longer I might have been out of that wheelchair in time to be standing for your weddings.'

'I couldn't wait,' James admitted. 'Not when

I realised how wrong we'd all been about that stupid pact to stay single for ever.'

Nobody was going to bother mentioning that the pact had been made in the wake of standing here with Mick like this that first time—when the bride had failed to arrive—but James made sure they weren't going to have time to even think about it.

'Plus,' he added swiftly, 'I didn't want Sarah to change her mind.'

'As if…' Mick scoffed. 'I hope you know how lucky you are, mate.'

'Oh, I do.' James nodded. He let his breath out in a contented sigh. 'I so do.'

His brothers might not agree, but he certainly did consider himself to be the luckiest man on earth. A husband, a father and a lover who also had his best friend to share the rest of his life with. Ivy had a little sister now called Holly—a name that had amused the rest of the family. Eddie had joked that they'd better not have another daughter or they'd be obliged to call her Mistletoe.

'Who would've thought you'd be the one to take the plunge first?' Eddie shook his head. 'It would have been polite to wait until after Jodie and I got round to it. I *was* the first one to break that pact, you know.'

'It's a long time ago,' James said calmly. 'Let

it go.' He caught Mick's glance and held it for a heartbeat. 'I do agree that some things are worth waiting for, though.'

Riley had asked Mick to marry her within days of arriving in Aberdeen and he'd apparently said he never wanted to have a day apart from her for the rest of his life but he wouldn't marry until he could walk down the aisle with her afterwards.

And here he was…albeit with a brother standing very close on each side of him…but it was their emotional support Mick wanted today, not anything physical. With Riley by his side for the long and hard journey, his recovery from his spinal injury had been inspirational.

The minister appeared and smiled at the Grisham brothers as she took her place. The music being played on the church organ changed to the traditional wedding march and all three brothers straightened and then turned as one, along with all the friends and family gathered, to watch the wedding party coming down the aisle.

Ella was the first, as the matron of honour. She had her gaze firmly on Mick and even from this distance James could see that she was about to lose the battle of keeping happy tears at bay.

The bridesmaids followed. Jodie was glowing in the late stages of her first pregnancy and she smiled at Mick, but then her gaze slid towards

Eddie as she arrived to take her place at the front of the church. James could feel the love in the way Eddie was looking back at his wife.

And now Sarah was almost within touching distance.

Looking *so* beautiful in her lovely dress.

His wife.

His love.

Sarah wasn't looking back at him, however. She had turned to see why the three flower girls—four-year-old Ivy, Ella's daughter Maggie, who was her best friend in the world, and her two-year-old sister, Holly, were no longer right behind her.

The three little cousins, who were wearing pretty matching dresses, were carrying small baskets full of rose petals that they were supposed to be sprinkling in front of the bride. Holly, however, had decided to sit down with her basket and play with her petals. Maggie was pointing at her as she tried to alert the adults to the issue but Ivy, who tended to be a bit bossy, was already trying to pull Holly back to her feet.

Behind them, Riley was coming down the aisle on the arm of Ella's husband, Logan. She was looking absolutely stunning in her white gown, holding a simple bunch of white flowers and…she was laughing at the obstacle in her way.

A ripple of laughter from everyone echoed from the walls of this ancient church. Riley held out a hand and Holly decided to allow her aunt to help her scatter a handful of petals. Sarah caught James's glance and he could see relief in her smile.

And pride.

And so much joy…

The minister was smiling just as broadly as everyone else as the wedding party settled into position to begin the exchange of solemn vows.

'Dearly beloved…' she began.

Sarah had Holly in her arms now and Ivy pressed against her leg. James could feel the presence of his brothers and the rest of his family surrounding him and…

And life didn't get any better than this, did it?

Dearly beloved, indeed…

He caught Sarah's glance. He didn't make a sound. He didn't even move his lips but he could still send the most important message.

Love you…

And it came straight back.

Love you too…

* * * * *

*If you missed the previous story in the
Daredevil Doctors duet, then check out*

Forbidden Nights with the Paramedic

*And if you enjoyed this story, check out
these other great reads from Alison Roberts*

Healed by a Mistletoe Kiss
The Italian, His Pup and Me
Fling with the Doc Next Door

All available now!